CW00865481

ULTIMATE ENDING

BOOK 10

MYSTERY
IN THE
MURKY DEEP

Check out the full

ULTIMATE ENDING BOOKS

Series:

Copyright © 2016 Ultimate Ending

www.UltimateEndingBooks.com

Cover design by Milan Jaram www.MilanJaram.com

Internal artwork by Jaime Buckley www.jaimebuckley.com

Enjoyed this book? Please take the time to leave a review on Amazon.

Dedicated to Caleb Schulte
You have so many adventures waiting for you!

Welcome to **Ultimate Ending,**
where YOU choose the story!

That's right – everything that happens in this book is a result of
decisions YOU make. So choose wisely!

But also be careful. Throughout this book you'll find tricks and traps,
trials and tribulations! Most you can avoid with common sense and a
logical approach to problem solving. Others will require a little bit of luck.
Having a coin handy, or a pair of dice, will make your adventure even more
fun. So grab em' if you got em'!

Along the way you'll also find tips, clues, and even items that can help
you in your quest. You'll meet people. Pick stuff up. Taking note of these
things is often important, so while you're gathering your courage, you
might also want to grab yourself a pencil and a sheet of paper.

Keep in mind, there are *many* ways to end the story. Some conclusions
are good... some not so good.
Some of them are even great!
But remember:

There is only *ONE*

ULTIMATE
ENDING!

Welcome to the Pacific Ocean!

You are JESSICA KWON, Dean of the Earth Sciences department at Stanford University. In addition to earning your Doctorates in Oceanography and Marine Biology, you've studied some of the most remote and incredible locations in the world: the barrier reef in Belize; sub-ice scavengers in Antarctica; even the inside of the Hawaiian volcanoes! Whenever there's a question about geology or oceanography, and someone needs to call in an expert, the expert they call is you.

But those days are long gone. As Dean of your own department, you don't get out much anymore. In fact, you haven't been on a research expedition in six years. You tried to take a week off to study penguin migration in Chile last summer, but a crisis at the University forced you to cancel. Face it: your days of excitement as a world adventurer are over.

Which is why it was quite a shock when two police officers suddenly arrested you in the middle of your lecture this morning.

"I don't understand," you say for the hundredth time from the back seat of the squad car. You're driving north along the coast, the dark waters of the Pacific Ocean to your left. "I don't understand why I've been arrested."

"You haven't been *arrested*, ma'am," says the officer in the front passenger seat, a dark-haired woman whose badge says Rodriguez. It's the hundredth time she's said that, too.

"Then what do you call this?" You tap the reinforced plexiglass barrier. "My students are probably panicking. As Dean, I only teach one class per semester, a six-hundred level course on marine chemistry. The midterm is next week."

The driver, a middle-aged man whose name you didn't see, chuckles. "Dude, that sounds tough. Like the kind of class I'd fall asleep in."

"You'd fall asleep in *any* class," Rodriguez says. She twists to face you. "Look, we know as little as you do. All we were told was to escort you there. I'm sorry for the inconvenience."

8

"When we get there, I'm going to tell them how unacceptable this is," you say.

Rodriguez gives you a pained look. "I'm sorry, ma'am. I really am. We're just following orders."

You cross your arms unhappily. "Where *are* we going, anyways?" It occurs to you nobody has mentioned that, yet.

"The San Francisco harbor," says the driver.

That makes your ears perk up. "Really?" Possibilities begin rolling through your head. Maybe there's a biological disaster. Or an influx of warm-water fish migrating inland, like two summers ago. For you to be grabbed in the middle of a lecture and driven straight there...

You blink at the sight of the Pacific Ocean. "Wait a minute. If we're going to the harbor, why are we this far west? We could have just taken the 101 north..."

Rodriguez whips her head toward her partner. "Seriously? You said you knew the way."

"I thought I did!"

"We were just transfered to the area," Rodriguez says to you. "Forgive my directionally-challenged partner."

"It's not my fault..." he mumbles.

"It's fine," you say. "Just merge onto the 280 when you come to it."

Honestly, you're still too excited about heading to the harbor to be mad. Your heart starts to race. What if it's a research expedition? There've been cases in the past where a scientist had to drop out of an expedition in an emergency, and replaced last-minute.

That still doesn't explain why they pretty much kidnapped you in the middle of your lecture. And it doesn't explain the secrecy.

The police cruiser hits traffic on the interstate. To your surprise, they flick on the siren and speed down the shoulder, lights blazing.

Whatever this is, it's important.

Your eyes widen as you eventually reach the harbor. Sitting in one of the docks is a long ship you recognize: the *RVS Aurora*. It's a research vessel primarily used in icy conditions. Does this mean the expedition is in the arctic circle? Or the antarctic?

The car drives through the security gate and down to the dock. Sure enough, it stops directly in front of the research vessel.

You're frozen in your seat looking out the front window. The *RVS Aurora* looms over you, a wall of burnished steel. A helicopter sits on the landing pad on its bow. The familiar feeling of preparing for an adventure, a tickle in the stomach and a rush of adrenaline, begins to take hold.

Someone clears their throat. You realize Officer Rodriguez has opened your door and is waiting for you to exit. The salty harbor breeze hits your face as you step out onto the platform.

A man in a shirt and tie is standing by the research vessel boarding ramp. He's holding a briefcase in one hand. He waves and comes over.

"I was afraid you wouldn't make it in time," he says. He has dark skin and thick-framed glasses, and he's wearing a tie with yellow rubber ducks on it.

"Lots of traffic on the 101," Rodriguez says, nudging her partner in the ribs.

"I'm Craig Albers." He sticks out his hand.

You shake it. "Pleasure to meet you, Mr. Albers–"

"Please, call me Craig," he says.

You continue as if he didn't say anything, "–but I'm going to insist you explain what's going on right now."

He smiles apologetically. "Yes, I'm afraid the secrecy was necessary." He pulls a file out of his briefcase and hands it to you.

You see your name, but the rest is a lot of legal-sounding text. "Can you tell me what this is, Mr. Alb–err, Craig?"

"Why, it's the United States Government emergency consultant form. The one where you volunteered to be used as an expert should a national emergency ever arise." He points. "Your signature is at the bottom."

Oh yeah. You remember now. You hold up the paper and say, "The date is also at the bottom. I signed it fifteen years ago!"

Craig takes the form and slides it back in his briefcase. "Thankfully it never expires!" he says cheerfully.

You decide it's not worth arguing. Your excitement is about to boil over. "So what's the emergency? Is it in the arctic, or antarctic?"

Craig blinks. "Pardon?"

"The *RVS Aurora*. It's an icebreaker. We're going somewhere with ice, right?"

That makes Craig laugh. "Oh no. We're not getting on the ship." He points. "We're borrowing its *helicopter*. We're traveling west. Into the Pacific."

10

"The Pacific," you repeat.

Craig smiles politely. "The Pacific Ocean."

"I know what you meant." You stare up at the research vessel. "So *where* in the Pacific Ocean are we going?"

"I'm afraid that's classified."

"And what will I be doing when I get there?"

He gives an apologetic shrug. "I can't tell you that, either. At least not until we're in international waters. But don't worry, it will all make sense once we're airborne! Now, if you'll follow me..."

He's waiting. What's it going to be?

To go with him, *FOLLOW TO PAGE 12*
If you don't like this one bit, turn him down *ON PAGE 33*

"Jackie," you say. "It's Jackie, and before you ask, I'm 100% positive."

Craig puts up his hands. "Okay, okay. I believe you!"

Sure enough, the same high-pitched *DING* sounds. The steps leading out of the pit glow softly. You follow them to the surface of the dome, where the next pit is illuminated by an invisible spotlight.

The moment your shoe touches the bottom of the pit, the voice returns, eager to quiz you:

"Mary's mother has four children: April, May, June, and... who?"

"Another name puzzle," Craig mutters.

What's the answer? Use the chart below to add up all the letters. Once you have the total, you can TURN TO THAT PAGE.

A = 1	F = 6	K = 11	P = 16	U = 21	Z = 26
B = 2	G = 7	L = 12	Q = 17	V = 22	Example:
C = 3	H = 8	M = 13	R = 18	W = 23	SHOP =
D = 4	I = 9	N = 14	S = 19	X = 24	19+8+15+16
E = 5	J = 10	O = 15	T = 20	Y = 25	= 58

If you have no idea, *GO TO PAGE 144*

12

"Okay, you've convinced me."

Craig chuckles without looking back. "That's good, because you didn't have a choice!"

One of those tall moving staircases is positioned at the edge of the dock, to allow direct access to the helicopter pad. You follow Craig inside and put on a helmet.

"Welcome aboard, ma'am."

The voice crackles inside your ear. It's the pilot speaking through a headset. You see a microphone in front of your own mouth, attached to the side of the helmet.

"So where are we going?" you ask him. He's wearing a navy uniform.

"West."

"Yeah, I'm familiar with the direction the *Pacific Ocean* is in," you say. "But where, specifically?"

"Apologies, ma'am, but that's not for me to say."

You lean back in your seat and clip your harness over your chest. "Am I ever going to get any answers?"

Craig frowns. "Of course you are. Just as soon as we're over international waters. I've been saying that all along..."

The sound of the rotors increases in pitch, and the helicopter jolts. You see the ship falling away beneath you. Here you go!

Get some answers *ON PAGE 15*

"Poland," you say. "Poland is the country that does not border–"
Before you can finish speaking, the voice cuts you off.

"Incorrect. Subject: failure. Please proceed to Dome Four."

You take a step back as the circle in the floor switches from green to red. Across the room, the door to the next dome slides open with a soft sound.
"So... we get to proceed even though my geography skills are rubbish?"
Craig shrugs. "Sort of. If we had passed..."
You shake your head. "Let's just go. Dome Three is where we need to get to anyways."
With confident strides, you move toward the door.

Enter Dome Four and *TURN TO PAGE 140*

14

You take a deep breath. "One. Two..."

"Three!"

You leap over the edge into open air. Immediately, you realize it's too far of a gap.

You're not going to make it!

You flail your arms as if that will help as you plummet. You smack into the side of the mountain, about ten feet short of the peak. Your momentum carries you down the side, sliding and scraping on the rock. It takes all your strength just to keep yourself from tumbling head over feet!

THWUNK.

You hit the ground, which sends shooting stars across your vision. A moment later you feel Craig land somewhere next to you. He begins to groan.

You're dizzy and disoriented, so you just lay there peacefully. You probably have a concussion. A deep feeling of failure comes over you. Not just failure for yourself, but for others. As if you're representing a huge group of people. And you let them down. You'll probably get out of the research habitat eventually, but you won't be able to continue, so this is...

THE END

You jolt awake violently, spinning your head all around. You're in the back of the helicopter. Craig is trying not to smile.

"Where are we?" you ask. There's nothing but dark blue in every direction.

"Over the Pacific," Craig says, as if that's obvious.

"You said you'd tell me where we're going as soon as we were over international waters."

"I did, but you fell asleep, and I didn't want to wake you." He shrugs. "Personally, I can never fall asleep in a moving vehicle. My brother is different. The moment a car or train starts moving he's snoring like–"

You cough to get his attention.

"Erm. Well. The coordinates we're heading toward are halfway between Hawaii and Alaska." He holds up a finger as you try to interrupt. "Yes, I know, there's nothing in that part of the Pacific. No land, at least. But there is a very special laboratory, one which we will–"

He's interrupted by the pilot. "Ship's coming into view now, sir."

"Ahh, perfect!" Craig leans forward to look out the front window. "There it is."

In the distance, outlined by the horizon, is a ship. You immediately recognize its long shape as a research vessel, with a flat landing pad on the bow, similar to the dozens of ships you've been on throughout your career.

"That's not a very large lab," you say. "That class of research vessel only has two test holds, each of them smaller than my office back on campus. I can't imagine what classified research you're doing out here, in the middle of nowhere."

The pilot twists around to look at Craig. "You didn't tell her?"

"She was sleeping."

You give Craig a blank look.

"*That* isn't the lab," he says. "That's just the way to access the lab. Well, the research habitat, is what we call it."

"I don't understand."

"The research habitat is *beneath* the ship. At the bottom of the Pacific Ocean."

Whaaaaat?

Find out more *ON PAGE 16*

16

"A research habitat. At the bottom of the Pacific Ocean," you say, deadpan.

"That's right."

"No, that's not right. That's *impossible*. The average depth of the Pacific ocean is 12,000 feet!"

He patiently listens to your protests. "This research habitat was constru–err, this habitat sits on a shelf high above the true ocean floor. The depth is far more manageable, I assure you. It will all be obvious soon."

The helicopter tilts, makes a full circle around the research vessel, then lands on the pad at its bow. The moment it touches down Craig jumps out, ducking to avoid the rotors.

You have no choice but to follow.

He leads you to the edge of the ship, where a cluster of men and women stand. Two small submarines are held in the air by massive winches. There's a loud *CRANK CRANK CRANK* sound as one of the submarines lowers to the edge of the ship. The hatch on the side opens.

"These are the other scientists," Craig says as they climb into the submarine. "There will be formal introductions once we reach the bottom."

The second submarine begins lowering, until it's at the same level as the first. The door opens, and a head sticks out. "Mr. Albers, you coming down?"

He grins with excitement. "Of course! This is the only fun part of my job."

At the first submarine, someone says, "One more seat open in here."

"You can go ahead," Craig tells you, striding toward sub number two. "I'll take the other one."

You look back and forth between the submarines, dangling in the air. Should you go with Craig and try to get info out of him? Or would the sub full of scientists have more answers?

To go with Craig, *DIVE TO PAGE 42*

If you'd rather talk to your fellow researchers, *TURN TO PAGE 23*

Once again, you do the math in your head. You double- and triple-check your answer to ensure you're correct.

"The answer is 17," you confidently say.

This time, a chime doesn't sound. For a very long, tense moment, you're afraid you got it wrong.

Then the stone slab jerks, and begins to descend into the mountain with the grinding sound of rock against stone. Within seconds the peak is a flat surface.

Except now there's a bridge on the other side, connecting to the third cone-shaped mountain behind the other two. The bridge is blue and looks like it's made of flattened laser beams. You can even see through it slightly.

Craig tests it with a shoe. "It feels solid."

"You mean you don't know?" you ask. "You sound like you're as clueless as me."

Instead of laughing at the joke, Craig gets a considering look on his face. "In a lot of ways, *yeah*, I am."

You say, "Also, if this is a research *habitat*, then where are the living quarters? The bedrooms, the kitchen? Where do people go to the bathroom? All I've seen in these domes are tests."

"That's a good question," Craig agrees. "But let's follow this before it disappears!" He speed walks down the laser bridge.

You have no choice but to follow.

Get to the next test by *GOING TO PAGE 70*

18

You consider the board for a long while. Knights are always confusing in chess because of the funky way they move.

"I think it goes here," you say, pointing.

Craig says, "Ehh, I'm not sure that's right."

His comment hits a nerve. "You don't think that's right? Well, why don't you contribute by telling me what this research habitat is for, and why we're even doing these dumb tests?"

"I told you," he says, "I don't know!"

"Then this is the move I'm making." You pick up the knight and place it heavily onto the spot.

You immediately know it's the wrong move. The board flashes red. You avoid looking in Craig's direction; you can tell he's giving you an *I told you so* stare.

"Well," you say, "it will probably let us try again, so–"

"*Test subjects: inadequate. Contain for later examination.*"

Something is happening. The Knight begins to grow, crushing the board beneath it. Within seconds it's the size of a real Knight, decked out in armor and riding a warhorse!

You and Craig back away slowly. The Knight follows. Pretty soon you're bumping against the wall of the dome. You glance over your shoulder and see a massive blue whale in the distance.

Craig holds up his palms and takes a step forward. "Listen, we don't want any trouble..."

The Knight pulls a weapon from its back and swings. It's a flail: a metal ball on the end of a long chain. It catches Craig in the gut, knocking him back.

"Oof!"

He groans on the floor. The Knight still blocks your way. There's no way for you to get past.

You wonder what sort of examination it's containing you for. Come to think of it, you wonder how a holographic chess piece could come to life and physically harm you in the first place! You have a thousand questions, and you won't get answers to any of them, because this is...

THE END

"The answer is–"

You don't even get a chance to say it before the voice interrupts you.

"Incorrect. Subject: failure. Proceed to next dome."

"But I didn't even give my answer yet! How do you know I was wrong?"

"It, uhh, does that sometime," Craig says. "From what I've read."

"It? What *it?*"

Craig shuffles his feet. "Well. The test protocol."

"Are you saying it read my mind?"

"I didn't say that." He looks toward the door. "Either way, it was the wrong answer. We should move on."

You take a deep breath to calm yourself. "Okay. Let's go."

Enter Dome Four *ON PAGE 140*

20

You're an oceanographer, and a Dean at Stanford. You've got this math problem *covered.*

"The answer is 20," you say after double-checking your work.

There's a soft chime in the air, vibrating all around you. It's obvious you got it right.

"Look," Craig says.

The carvings on the stone slab begin to swirl and morph, as if it were made of clay. When they stop there's a new problem:

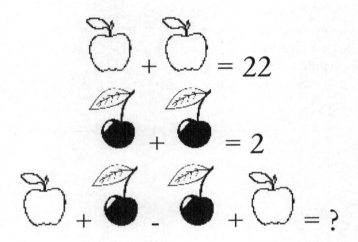

You touch the stone surface. "I don't understand how it could do that. It feels solid!"

Craig nods. "There's a lot we don't understand. That's why *you* are here. You and the other scientists, I mean."

"Well, they're not here now, so I guess it's up to us." You examine the problem.

Do you know the answer to the math problem? If so, *TURN TO THAT PAGE*
If you don't know, that's okay too. Instead, *GO TO PAGE 59*

You rearrange the names in your head based on the clues. If Hanley is behind David...

"David," you blurt out. "I think David is at the front of the line."

A piercing siren stings your ears for a moment. Even before the voice speaks you know you've guessed wrong.

"INCORRECT. Subject: failure. Proceed to next dome."

Craig says nothing as you climb out of the pit. The other two pits remain dark. You wonder if those would have been any easier.

"It's not your fault, Jessica," Craig says. "I had no idea what it was either."

"Being an Oceanographer isn't helping me much down here," you say.

Craig nods. "Yeah. Nobody has had much luck..."

The door to Dome Three stands open at the end of the room. "At least we're almost there," you say. "Let's go!"

Hey, you've reached Dome Three. That's good, right? *TURN TO PAGE 130*

22

After a few seconds, you grin to yourself. "It's a trick problem. You both add *and* subtract the second symbol, which cancel each other out."

A grin splits Craig's freckled face. "So the answer is 22!"

"Yep!"

Again, the soft bell-like chime makes all the molecules in the air vibrate. It's a pleasing feeling, even though the problems aren't that difficult for you.

You realize Craig is holding up his palm for a high-five. You can't help but smile and smack your palm against his.

The stone symbols swirl and change again. This time you try touching them while it happens, but something stops you. It's as if the air in front of the stone slab has thickened into a shield. Within seconds it's gone, and a new problem is waiting to be solved.

$$\text{🍎} + \text{🍎} + \text{🍎} = 30$$
$$\text{🍎} + \text{🍒} + \text{🍒} = 20$$
$$\text{🍒} - \text{🍌} = 3$$
$$\text{🍎} + \text{🍒} + \text{🍌} = ?$$

±

Do you know the answer to the math problem? If so, *TURN TO THAT PAGE* If you don't know, don't panic. Instead, *GO TO PAGE 59*

Craig's just a guy in a suit. The scientists are where the real info is! You rush over to their sub and climb inside.

The submarine is *tiny*. It's no bigger than your bathroom, and it's crammed with people. There are six chairs mounted to the walls, five of which are occupied. You settle into the only open chair, next to a big guy with his arms crossed. He snorts at you. "Astronomer? Or chemist?"

"Uhh... excuse me?"

He gestures at the others. "We're all in different fields. I'm a geologist. Frank over there is a *physicist*. Marlene is a literature professor. Literature!" Marlene makes a face.

"So, I was trying to guess what you're an expert in. What is it?"

"Oceanography," you say. "Dean at Stanford."

"Well la-di-da," the man mutters. "Someone who actually sounds relevant to this crazy research habitat."

The submarine jerks in the air, sways back and forth, and then plunges into the water with a muted *SPLASH*. The view out the porthole changes from sky to water as it descends.

"You sound like you haven't been down to it before," you say.

"None of us have," Frank says. "Just the submarine pilot."

"I heard there's a similar habitat in the Atlantic Ocean," says another.

The driver turns around from the cockpit. "You'll see. The habitat's made up of five geometric domes. We discovered that each dome houses different tests to gauge–"

He cuts off as the entire submarine shudders. There's a popping noise, and a pressure in your ears.

"I'm... losing internal pressure," the driver says. "Mayday! Mayday! I've lost all buoyancy! Sub two, we need assistance..."

"What do we do?" Marlene asks.

"Open the hatch!" cries Frank. "We've only been diving for a minute. We should be close to the surface!"

"You're the oceanographer," says the geologist next to you. There's panic in his voice. "What should we do?"

To open the hatch and try to swim to the surface, *RISE TO PAGE 73*
If you'd rather stay put and wait for help, *STAY ON PAGE 24*

24

"Let's all stay calm," you say. "We're just passengers here. We shouldn't be trying to do things on our own."

That seems to placate the others. It feels awfully crowded in the sub—you're crammed elbow to elbow. There are a lot of red lights flashing in the cockpit. For the first time in your life you feel claustrophobic. And that includes the time you went cave-diving in Belize!

Eventually the driver turns to face the cabin. "We've lost all buoyancy controls, but that's okay. Sub two is coming around. They'll let us borrow a tube of sealant gel and we should be all set."

Everyone visibly relaxes. The lights in the cockpit are flashing, but at least there's a plan.

You see the other submarine approach through the porthole on the opposite wall, just next to the hatch. It pulls alongside you like you're sitting in a parking lot. There's a *THUD THUD THUD* sound, like a woodpecker is hammering the outside of the hull. For a moment you're not sure if you should be worried.

"Okay, they're connected," the driver calls. "Open the hatch!"

The geologist jumps to it before you can. A few turns of the wheel and the door swings open.

There's a short tunnel connecting the two submarines. A few feet on the other side is Craig's suited shape, waving pleasantly. He tosses a tube of what looks like toothpaste, which you catch with both hands.

"Here you go. Should be all you need."

You look inside his sub longingly. It's so *empty* compared to sub one! You'd have plenty of room to stretch your legs. You even think you can feel a cool breeze coming from the other side.

They're about to close the hatch.

To stay put like a good passenger, *GO TO PAGE 26*
If you'd rather go with Craig on sub one, *JUMP ACROSS TO PAGE 89*

The driver in the cockpit starts punching buttons. "I copy you, sub one. Halting descent and coming around to assist."

"Are they okay?" you ask Craig.

"I don't know." He's holding onto the armrest so tight his fingers are turning white. Something tells you the suited man is regretting coming along for the ride.

Though the waters on the other side of the glass are murky, you can see a cone of light some distance away. It grows as you approach. You can see the other scientists through the portholes, waving for help.

"What's the problem?" your driver says.

"Seal broke on one of the buoyancy valves," comes the voice on the radio. "We're losing pressure fast, and we can't control our depth!"

The driver turns around and points. "You, miss! Above your head is an emergency toolkit. There's sealant gel in there." Then, to the radio, he says, "Sub one, we've got what you need. We'll extend the docking connector and hand it over."

"Whew," Craig says. "Glad it was an easy fix."

But the driver turns back to you. "I'm going to need one of you to operate the docking connector."

"Wha, what? Why can't you do it?"

"I'm keeping our sub even with theirs. I can't be at two places at once! Now come on, it's easy–just use the joystick to extend it toward their hatch. Come on!"

Craig looks as pale as a ghost, and hasn't moved at all. As a world renowned oceanographer, you're going to have to take over.

You unclip your seatbelt and jump to the docking controls. There's a computer screen and a camera to help you line it up, but the subs keep moving back and forth! You're going to have to time it perfectly.

And it's going to take some luck.

Roll a die! (if you don't have one, pick a random number from 1 to 6)

If you roll a 1, 2, 3, 4, or 5, *JUMP TO PAGE 49*
If you roll a 6, *INSTEAD GO TO PAGE 58*

26

The connection between the two subs doesn't look very sturdy: it's made of some sort of flimsy plastic composite, and it crinkles loudly from the pressure around it. No thank you.

Geologist closes the hatch, twisting the wheel until it will go no further. While he does that, you take the tube of sealant gel to the driver.

"Awesome. *Awesome.* Nice job back there." He hands the tube back to you. "See that crack on the floor, behind my seat?"

You bend down to examine the problem. "Yeah. I can feel the air coming out!"

"Oh man," moans the geologist. "*Oh man.*"

The driver nods without facing you. "That's right. The buoyancy tanks are leaking air into here, screwing up the descent. Just squeeze a line of gel along the seam. Make sure the bead is uniform."

You pop off the cap and puncture the end with a fingernail. Moving with expert deftness, you run the end of the tube along the crack, squeezing the tube at the same time. Just like putting out sea crab bait!

The gel bubbles as it fights the escaping air, but quickly grows still. You can practically see it hardening before your eyes.

"Did you do it yet?" The driver asks. "I'm still—no, hold on a second. *Yes.* There we go! We're stabilizing!"

The cramped cabin erupts in cheers. Geologist smacks you on the back so hard you nearly fall.

"Research Vessel Gamma? This is sub one. We've resolved our issue and are returning back to the surface."

It takes you a moment to realize what he said. "Wait, why the surface?"

"That gel is working for now, but it's only a temporary fix. It probably won't hold when we're twenty atmospheres down." His tone changes. "Roger than, Gamma. See you soon."

The other scientists are relieved to be escaping their small taste of the ocean. You feel much the same—though at the same time, you wonder what was down in the research habitat. Maybe someday you'll find out. But for now, all you'll find back on the surface vessel is...

THE END

The hawk room is decorated with–you guessed it–a black sculpture of a hawk. Its wings are spread wide and its mouth is open in a silent screech.

You have two options.

To the south is a door with a raven carved above.

To the west is a door with a peacock carving.

You glance around at the open air above the maze. "Maybe we should have left the dome flooded. Then we could just swim above it."

"Huh. Yeah, I guess so." Craig takes off his glasses and cleans them on his shirt. "Which way do you want to go?"

To enter the raven room, *FLY TO PAGE 82*

If you want to walk through the peacock door, *GO TO PAGE 165*

28

"This is the correct move," you say, sliding the Knight two spaces forward and one to the side. "It checks the King, *and* blocks his escape. Checkmate!"

Again, the board flashes green around the outside. You grin in spite of yourself. These tests are actually pretty fun!

Craig wipes sweat from his forehead. "This is a *lot* more exciting than sitting in my office. I never get to take part in stuff like this."

The board has already changed. It's more complex than ever, now.

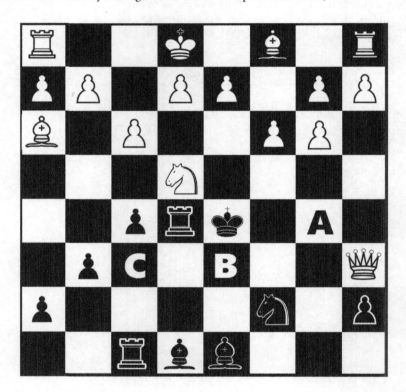

Which piece do you move, and where?

To move the white Queen to square **A**, *GO TO PAGE 30*
To move the white Queen to square **B**, *GO TO PAGE 46*
To move the white Queen to square **C**, *GO TO PAGE 38*
To move the white Knight to square **B**, *GO TO PAGE 78*
To move the white Knight to square **C**, *GO TO PAGE 181*

You flail around as you fall, gloved fingers scraping through the sandy cliff face. That slows you down, but not by much. Your suit weighs enough to carry you down as if pulled by a lasso.

"Craig!" you cry out. "Craig!"

You tumble through the water, head over feet. You can see the cone of his headlamp above you, then it disappears, then you see it again, smaller. You're falling away. How far is it to the bottom? The thought terrifies you.

Just as you begin to scream, something strikes you in the back. For a few terrible seconds you can't breathe as the wind is knocked out of you. But your lungs start working again, and you cautiously get to your feet.

You're not on the ocean floor–you're on some sort of ledge in the cliff face, five feet wide. And strangely enough, it's not natural. It's perfectly square, and made of the same black material as the rest of the research habitat.

"Jessica? Are you okay? I can see your light. Jessica, say something!"

"I'm okay," you say, glancing upward. His headlamp cone isn't too far above. Maybe 40 or 50 feet. "I'm on a ledge down here." You pause. "Hey, there's a door!"

"A door?"

It's outlined against the cliff face, obviously man-made. You take a step forward and it slides open, revealing a small room inside.

"Yeah, a door," you repeat. "I think it's an airlock inside."

"Inside what? That's way below the dome!"

You shrug, though he can't see the motion. "I don't know, but unless you have another way for me to climb back up to you..."

Craig sighs into the microphone, then begins to half-climb, half-fall down the cliff face. He lands next to you with a thump.

The two of you step into the airlock. The door closes automatically, and then there's a weird pressurized feeling on the outside of the suit. Then the water begins draining from the room, the water line falling below your helmet. As soon as it reaches your feet you pull apart your suit. Craig is already out of his too.

The door in front of you opens.

What's inside? Find out *ON PAGE 172*

30

"The Queen's the most powerful piece," you start to say.

"Not always!" Craig interrupts.

"In this case, though, it is." You move the Queen across the board.

Immediate, the board flashes red. You hear the hum of electricity in the air. It feels like a lightning strike is about to happen.

"Test subjects: critical failure. Eliminate."

"Eliminate!" Craig looks around. "What does it mean by eliminate?"

Both exits from the dome are closed. And you can't just smash the glass. What do you do?

The chess board warps and changes. Eight of the Pawns grow rapidly before your eyes until they're the same size as you. They're not armored, but they *do* have swords. Blank-faced and stoic, they quickly spread out, surrounding you and Craig.

In the back of your head, you're wondering what kind of a research facility this really is. You want to blame Craig for bringing you, but you're afraid to speak. As the Pawns close in, you accept that you've probably reached...

THE END

"Dustin!" you blurt out.

Craig says, "Yeah! It's Dustin!"

A piercing siren stings your ears for a moment. Even before the voice speaks you know you've guessed wrong.

"INCORRECT. Subject: failure. Proceed to next dome."

You're crestfallen. "I thought for sure that was right. You thought so too!"

Craig makes an apologetic face. "Well, I just wanted to agree with you. You were so confident! I figured it had to be right."

You deliberately ignore the other two pits, which remain dark. The door to Dome Three is ahead, open wide, showing the tunnel beyond.

"What matters is that we've reached our goal," you say. "Even if we did fail the test. Let's go find out what happened to Dome Three!"

Your words seem to lift Craig up. He smiles and leads the way on eager feet.

Approach Dome Three by *FLIPPING TO PAGE 130*

32

The dolphin room has an ornate statue of a dolphin standing in the center, the kind of thing you'd find as a fountain in a water park, except it's black and spongy and doesn't have water shooting out of its mouth. You take a moment to admire it.

"I wonder what the point of these statues is," you say out loud.

"Decoration?"

You shake your head. "Yeah, but *why*? It seems like there's some other reason."

Craig shrugs. "Let's focus on where to go next. I'm starting to miss my computer desk."

To the north is the maze entrance.

To the east is a door with a dog carving.

To the south is a door with a cat statue.

To the west is a door with what looks like coral carved into the wall.

Go north *ON PAGE 128*
Turn east by *FLIPPING TO PAGE 47*
Head south *ON PAGE 65*
Wander west *TO PAGE 40*

You take a deep breath and shake your head. Craig doesn't see it because he's walking away, expecting you to follow.

"After careful consideration, I'm going to have to pass," you say.

He turns around. For some reason he looks amused. "Pass?"

"You're going to need to find someone else. I'm the *Dean*. I cannot simply disappear for an extended period of time just because–"

"You mistake me, Miss Kwon," Craig says, still wearing that not-smile on his face. "You have no choice. This is a matter of national security. If you were to try to walk away from this you will be brought up on several charges: breach of contract, contempt of a government officer, treason."

"*Treason?*"

He nods gravely. "Feel free to test the boundary of my power. I assure you, it is limitless." He continues walking toward the helicopter.

You reluctantly follow. Treason?

Where is he taking you?

A movable staircase on the dock leads directly to the helicopter pad. The rotors start slowly spinning as you follow Craig inside. He hands you a helmet, which muffles the sound of the engine spinning up. A microphone sticks out in front of your mouth.

"Now will you tell me where we're going?"

He smiles apologetically. "Soon enough!"

You turn away from him, annoyed, and watch the ship fall beneath you. You're already taking off!

Head west *TO PAGE 15*

34

"This way!" you cry, heading through the east doorway like your life depends on it. Craig doesn't argue.

The sound of fluttering wings and the scrape of talons on the floor tell you that the ostrich is following. You know you can't hope to fight the bird–they're huge, and adept at using their legs and beak as weapons. While sprinting down the hall you search your memory for anything that might help. Why did you have to choose marine biology instead of a focus on avian biology?

You finally burst into the next room, which bears a statue of a flock of stone doves. There's also a locker-type structure against the wall. Aside from that, there's nothing.

It's a dead end.

"Look out!" Craig blurts. Without looking, you throw yourself to the side. Long feathers fly past you as the ostrich misses its charge. You can feel the heavy stomping in the floor as it continues on. Maybe if you get up you can return the way you–

CRASH!

The ostrich slams into the wall of the dome. It bounces off cartoonishly, falling onto its back. It jumps up, shakes its head, and then sprints back the way it came–completely ignoring you and Craig.

"Hey! How about that!" you say.

"No. How about that," Craig says, pointing to the wall. A long crack mars the glass, spreading and spiderwebbing into two, three, four individual cracks. Your ears pop as water begins dribbling down the side.

Any moment and it will all crash inward.

What are you going to do?

To follow the ostrich to safety, *RUN TO PAGE 186*
If you want to check the lockers, *HURRY TO PAGE 87*

You're in the bottom of the pit. Unlike Dome One, there aren't any screens. In fact, there's nothing down there at all except a blue circle on the floor. Not sure what else to do, you step into the circle.

The acoustics are crazy here. You can hear the echo of your own breathing in surround-sound! You can sense Craig standing behind you.

A voice cuts the air, quiet and loud at the same time. It's the same calm, robotic-sounding voice from the first dome. After each sentence it speaks, there's a notable pause.

"Six in a line, six they do meander: David, Dustin, Hanley, Jackie, Mookie, and Xander.

Hanley is behind David and Mookie.
Mookie is in front of Dustin.
Jackie is behind Hanley, Xander and Dustin.
Dustin is in front of Jackie and Xander.
Xander is in front of Hanley and David.
Xander is behind Mookie.

In order to prove the worth of your kind, who is at the front of the line?"

The last word hangs in the air.

"Ohh, I get it," you say. It's like a word puzzle! You have to use the clues to determine the order.

"So... what's the answer?" Craig asks.

Can you use logic to figure out who is at the front of the line? You might need paper and pencil to visualize it!

If it's **David**, *GO TO PAGE 21*
If it's **Dustin**, *GO TO PAGE 31*
If it's **Hanley**, *GO TO PAGE 41*
If it's **Jackie**, *GO TO PAGE 51*
If it's **Mookie**, *GO TO PAGE 61*
If it's **Xander**, *GO TO PAGE 71*

36

The statue in the center of the ostrich room is huge, a reminder of just how big real ostriches are. It's so life-like, with its feathers all ruffled and its beak open...

Before you realize what you're doing, you touch its surface. And in the blink of an eye, the black, spongy material fades away like mist. You're left standing in front of what looks like a *real* ostrich, with black feathers and a pink neck and eyes like dark marbles.

The eyes blink, and it cocks its head at you in a distinctively bird-like manner. "*AHH-KAWWW.*"

The sound is unlike anything you've ever heard, and you stumble backwards instinctively. The bird takes one tentative step forward, testing its legs. Then another.

Craig grabs your arm and helps you up. "It was just a statue," he whispers. "How'd you do that?"

"I think it was real, but that black material was encasing it somehow. Like it was frozen. What I'm *really* curious about is how an ostrich got all the way down here..."

The bird flaps its huge wings in an aggressive manner, and begins high-stepping toward you. You seem to recall that ostriches are *awfully* fast.

There are four doors out of this room. The ostrich is blocking the door to the north, the way you came.

To the east is a door with a dove carving. You can tell it borders the exterior of the dome.

To the south is a door with a vulture carving.

To the west is a room with a pigeon carving above the door.

"We need to *go*," Craig says. The ostrich begins to charge.

To flee east, *RUN TO PAGE 34*
If you want to go south, *HEAD TO PAGE 45*
If west seems safest, *DART TO PAGE 50*

The statue in the center of this room is like something out of a fantasy novel: the body of a lion, but wings and head of a bird. As you approach you realize just how *big* it is. Even sitting down, it must be twenty feet tall. You're glad it's just a statue.

"Hey, look at this."

Craig's pointing at the floor behind the statue. You stare down at the words, carved into the floor:

*The way to be free
lies with eights, or...*

There was more written, but it's not longer legible.

"Okay... whatever that means."

You wrinkle your face. "Hmm. I wonder who scratched that."

"Whoever it was, it doesn't help us anymore," Craig says. "This is a dead end."

You see that he's right: the only way back is north. Your eyes linger on the west wall for a moment–you thought there was a door there, but you must have been mistaken.

Think about the clue and *TURN TO PAGE 39*

38

You slide the piece across the board. "I believe that's check–"

BZZZAP!

An arc of electricity shoots off the piece and hits you in the finger. "Oww!" It feels like you smashed your funny bone into a wall. Your entire hand has gone numb!

"Test failure. Proceed to Dome Four."

You wonder where the robotic voice is coming from. But whatever it is, it's turned the green circle in the floor red.

"If we failed," you say, "then why do we get to advance? What's the point of these tests?"

"I wish I could tell you," Craig says.

You take a deep breath and let it out slowly. "I should be back at Stanford right now."

"I should be sitting in my office filling out paperwork," Craig says, "but we're both here now, so we might as well make the best of it. At least it's exciting, right?"

Instead of answering, you stride toward the door marked DOME FOUR. The tunnel feels small compared to the cavernous dome.

Enter Dome Four *ON PAGE 140*

"I'm telling you," Craig says, "that's not a weasel. It's a ferret."

The statue is small, about the length of a tube sock. You shrug. "Whatever you say."

"I had a pet ferret when I was a boy. I know one when I see one."

"I said okay!"

To the north is a door with a dog carved above.

To the south is a door with a gryphon carving.

To the west is a door with a cat carving.

"Are we on the right track?" you mutter.

"Heck if I know."

North? *SCURRY TO PAGE 47*
Walk south *ON PAGE 37*
Go west by *FLIPPING TO PAGE 65*

40

The coral reef statue in this room of the maze is stunning: there are staghorn coral, pillar coral, and mushroom coral all made of calcium. Black coral and maze-like brain coral. Even though the statue is colorless, the oceanographer in you sees the entire thing in vibrant shades of yellow, orange, and purple. It takes up most of the room.

"This is incredible," you say. "Why is this here?"

"That's a *very* good question." Craig bobs his head. "Very good. Yes."

You peel your eyes from the structure. There are two ways to go.

To the east is a doorway with a dolphin carved over the door.

To the south is an opening with a carving of a killer whale.

Go east   *TO PAGE 32*
Or, head south   *TO PAGE 48*

"If Dustin is in front of both Jackie *and* Xander," you mutter.

"And Mookie is in front of Dustin," Craig adds.

"It's Hanley. It's gotta be." You raise your voice. "Hanley!"

There's a long moment of silence. When the robotic voice finally speaks you can almost sense disappointment in its tone.

"INCORRECT. Critical failure of logic tests. Subjects being quarantined for further study."

"Quarantined?" you and Craig say at the same time, just as a shadow drifts over you.

You realize it's coming from the floor of the dome above you. Some sort of cover is sliding into place above the pit!

You rush up the steps but it's too late. The metal ceiling slides into place with a hollow *BANG*, plunging the pit in darkness.

You're trapped and out of options, which means this is...

THE END

42

You jog across the boat to catch up with Craig. He's already inside the sub, so you duck your head through the hatch.

The space is about as large as your bathroom back home, with six chairs arranged in pairs on three walls. The fourth wall is another hatch leading to the cockpit, where there's a beautiful glass bubble showing the sky. Smaller portholes are spaced throughout.

Craig sits in the first chair and buckles himself in. He smiles at seeing you join. "I thought you'd rather make the trip with your fellow scientists."

"I'm still not sick of you, yet."

You grab a seat across from him and clip your own seatbelt together. The driver in the cockpit begins talking on the radio to someone, and the whole submarine begins to sway as it's swung out over the water. With what feels like reckless speed it drops into the water with a muted *SPLASH.*

"That's my favorite part," Craig grins. "Way more exciting than the office."

The submarine begins to descend. There's not much to see through the cockpit, so you turn to Craig.

"Tell me about this research habitat."

He takes off his glasses and cleans them with his tie. "Well. The habitat is made up of five geometric domes, each with different testing equipment inside. They're connected in a ring shape, with tunnels between them. It's all very high-tech..."

"Yeah, but what's the *purpose* of the lab? What are we testing?"

"That's a complicated question," he says slowly. "The easiest I can explain it is–"

He cuts off as the radio in the cockpit blares to life. "Submarine number two! Attention, submarine number two! We are experiencing catastrophic pressure failure. Mayday, mayday. I repeat, we are experiencing..."

"That's the first sub," Craig says. "They're in trouble!"

Catastrophic pressure failure? See what you can do *ON PAGE 25*

"Wait, there's some trick to this question," Craig says.

"I agree, the obvious answer seems *too* obvious." You think for a moment. "Oh! What if the order is different? The other child is *March*?"

"Huh?"

"Like, the children's names are *March*, April, May, and June. Right?"

"I don't think that's–" Craig is cut off by the robotic voice, which now sounds more annoyed than calm, as if you've been wasting its time:

"Incorrect answer. Defective subjects likely. Disposing."

"Uhh. What does *that* mean?"

Craig looks down. "I feel something rumbling in the ground."

Suddenly the floor opens in half. You scream as you plummet into darkness.

SPLASH!

You land in water, which at first is a relief compared to free-falling. Then you open your eyes.

There's a half-sphere of light in front of you, about half a football field away. It takes you a minute to realize what it is: one of the domes!

You're outside the dome! In the ocean!

You kick and thrash around, trying to swim toward the dome, even though you have no idea how you'll get back inside. The water is so cold! You quickly lose strength, and then your vision goes black.

You open your eyes to see Craig.

You're on the floor of the sub: the same one that took you down to the research habitat in the first place! But how...

"The sub was just returning when it saw us floating," Craig responds to your confused look. "Lucky timing, huh? We're heading back to the surface now."

You try to answer, but a fountain of water comes up. You roll over and spit the water out on the floor, staring at the metal. Taking it all in. You're lucky to be back where it's safe, but you won't have another chance to investigate the research vessel. Which, of course, means this is...

THE END

44

The knight advances quickly. Instinct wins out over battle tactics–you're just an Oceanographer!–and you jump out of the way.

But his reflexes are too good. He follows you easily, swinging his sword with lightning speed. He delivers three quick blows, to your head and arm and shield, knocking you on your back. Your head striking the ground sends a flash of light across your eyes.

You stare at the ceiling of the dome until the knight's face blocks the view, staring down. He points his sword at your face and gives a final nod of courtesy.

Before he can finish you off, though, he suddenly disappears. All you see is the ceiling of the dome.

Craig is there in a hurry, pulling you to your feet. "You were so close!"

The three screens have already turned off, returning the platform to boring normalcy. A voice cuts the air, seemingly coming from everywhere all at once, like it's speaking in your imagination:

"Subject: failure. Proceed to next dome."

Across the room, by the door to Dome Two, the door suddenly opens.

"Wait, I thought I lost," you say. "I thought I had to pass these tests to proceed."

Craig shrugs. "I'm not sure how it works. Let's just go, shall we?"

You give the other platform a final disappointing look. Wondering what test would have occurred there, you follow Craig to the exit.

It could have been worse. Advance to Dome Two *ON PAGE 120*

You take off through the south doorway. The sculpture of the vulture hanging over the door seems to follow you with hollow, unseeing eyes.

"*AHH-KAWW,*" the ostrich screeches as it pursues you. Its long, thin legs kick high into the air as it runs. You *don't* want to find out how much that hurts.

The vulture room has only one other doorway. One option for escape. Taking care to avoid the statue in the middle, you head for the gap.

But the door slides down from the ceiling, blocking it off. It's now a seamless, spongy wall!

Uh oh!

You turn around. The ostrich is taking its time now, as if it realizes it has you cornered. It swivels its head at you, then at Craig.

"Craig," you say. "So *why* is there an ostrich in a habitat at the bottom of the ocean?"

"I don't know, because we didn't build this habitat," he says in exasperation. "We *found it.*"

You want to ask what he means, but the ostrich is approaching. It has stubby black claws on the ends of its toes, not quite as sharp as talons but dangerous nonetheless. *Is my fate really at the hands of an ostrich at the bottom of the ocean?* you think to yourself, just before bracing for...

THE END

46

After careful consideration–chess is a thinking game, after all–you move the Queen. "Checkmate."

"Yeah!" cries Craig.

The board flashes green around the edges three times, then disappears entirely. Across the room, one of the other two circles in the floor changes from red to green, beckoning you.

"Hopefully this test is just as easy," you say.

The two of you walk over to the second circle. This one has no table. It's completely empty except for the outer circle. Tentatively, you step inside.

Immediately, the calm voice returns to your thoughts:

"Poland, France, and Italy. Which country DOESN'T border Germany?"

"Seriously? A geography test?" What is this, grade school?

"Uhh," Craig says.

"Why are you quizzing my knowledge of European countries? How does that have to do with anything at all?"

"I wish I knew," Craig said. "Maybe it will make sense when we get to Dome Three?"

You sigh. Better get this over with.

Do you know which country does not border Germany?

If it's **Poland**, *TURN TO PAGE 13*
To guess **France**, *GO TO PAGE 19*
If the answer is **Italy**, *FLIP TO PAGE 90*

"Hey!" you cry out, running into the middle of the dog room.

"What?"

You stop in from of the statue. It's a German Shepherd, sitting on its haunches and smiling with its mouth open. "He looks just like my dog."

"Oh." Craig shifts his feet. "What did you... is he..."

There's a note of question in his voice. "Don't worry. My neighbor is dog-sitting him while I'm gone. Hopefully it's just for another day or two." You let a bit of scorn trickle into your voice.

Craig holds up his hands. "Hey, you and me both. Which way should we go?"

To the south is a door with a weasel or ferret carving.

To the west is a door with a dolphin carved into the wall.

If you want to head south, *GO TO PAGE 39*
If you would prefer to go west, *TURN TO PAGE 32*

48

The statue of the killer whale is oppressively large in such a small space. Who would have built this here? You can barely even walk around it.

"Killer whales are the apex predators of the ocean, you know."

"Apex predator?"

"You know, an alpha predator. Hypercarnivore." He gives you a blank look. "The top of the food chain?"

"Ohh, right," he says. Then: "Wait. It's not sharks?"

"Nope!" You smile knowingly. It's your favorite fun fact to tell students. "Killer whales are the wolves of the sea. They hunt in packs, and easily kill great white sharks. They're at the top."

"Except for humans," Craig points out.

"Well, humans don't quite count, because we're not native to that type of biome. We only visit."

Craig shrugs. Not everyone appreciates your knowledge of ocean life.

To the north is a doorway with intricate coral carved on the wall.

To the west is a passage with a long, pointed swordfish carved above.

Go north by *JUMPING TO PAGE 40*
Alternatively, go west *TO PAGE 56*

You squint at the computer screen. The target is a square hatch on the other submarine. It *should* be easy to line up, but because both subs are still falling through the water, it's tougher than you expected.

"Can you keep us steady?" you yell.

The driver says, "I'm trying!"

You're running out of time. You can see the scientists through the porthole, waving and calling for help. You have to help them!

The hatch lines up, and you throw the joystick forward. There's a soft *THUD* that you feel as much as hear. For a long moment everything is still.

"Open it up, and be ready to toss them the sealant," the driver says. "An undersea soft-dock is dangerous. I want to get disconnected as soon as possible!"

You grab the hatch wheel and pull it open. The first turn is the toughest, but it gets progressively easier. Suddenly the entire door opens outward.

The tube connecting the two subs is *tiny*, barely big enough for a person to crawl through. The walls are made of a flexible carbon material, and bend dangerously with the pressure of the water pushing down.

The hatch on the other side opens. Your ears pop, a sign that their pressure is failing. You toss the tube of sealant gel toward them, they flash you a smile of thanks, and then they close their hatch.

You quickly do the same. There's a soft rumble as the docking tube disconnects. The driver lets out a long sigh.

"Nice job." His tone changes to something more professional. "Sub one. Confirm your status please."

Did it work? *FIND OUT ON PAGE 62*

50

You run through the west door because, well, why not? It's not as if you know which way to go.

The ostrich is right on your heels as you enter the next room. Not slowing, you pick a door at random. One with another type of bird carving. You're moving too fast to tell.

You fly through rooms of the maze, each one a blur as you put distance between yourself and the ostrich. Penguin room. Eagle room. One with a long-legged, wide-winged bird: an egret, or maybe a stork. You soon stop looking because it's taking away your focus.

Eventually something grabs your arm. For a brief, terrifying moment you think it's the ostrich... until you remember ostriches don't have fingers.

You let Craig's grip slow you down and glance over your shoulder. The ostrich is gone.

"The ostrich is gone," he says, as if it's obvious.

You stop completely. You're in a room with a snake statue in the middle, coiled and ready to strike. You take a few seconds to catch your breath.

"Well okay then," you say.

Craig wanders into the next room. As you follow, the doorway behind you closes shut. The movement was strange: one moment there was an opening, and the next the walls were closing in. Now you can't tell there was ever a door there at all.

There's a peacock in this room. "That seems familiar," Craig says. "I think..." He walks through into the next room.

And what do you know? It's the entrance to the maze.

You're back at the beginning.

It's better than being pummeled by an angry ostrich! *LEAF TO PAGE 128*

"The right answer is Jackie," you say. "Well. I think."

"You *think*?" Craig says.

Before you can defend your guess, the voice fills the air. It seems surprisingly upset.

> "*INCORRECT. Critical failure of logic tests. Subjects being quarantined for further study.*"

"Quarantined?" you and Craig say at the same time, just as a shadow drifts over you.

You realize it's coming from the floor of the dome above you. Some sort of cover is sliding into place above the pit!

You sprint up the stairs, pushing Craig ahead of you. He's scrambling forward as fast as he can, which isn't very quick in his business attire. He makes it through, but as you follow the door to the pit closes on your ankle.

"Ahhh!"

You cry out, but your ankle isn't crushed: it's merely pinned between the metal and the edge of the pit. You're trapped!

Craig frantically runs around the dome to look for a way to free you, but it's a fruitless effort. You probably should have taken your time on the puzzle, because your wrong guess has caused you to reach...

THE END

52

"If we move the Queen vertically, and take the pawn, the King won't be in check," you say.

"Uh huh."

"And if we go diagonally, to this square, the King will capture the Queen. Check, but not checkmate."

"Definitely."

"So we need to move the Queen horizontally. By going *here*-" you move the Queen to the edge of the board, "-we will put the King in checkmate!"

The moment you let go of the piece, the border of the chess board flashes blue in a decisively positive sign. You smile to yourself.

Craig lets out a long breath. "You know, at first I was regretting coming inside the research habitat. But now I'm having fun! This is exciting, no matter the danger."

"Hold on a second," you say. "What danger?"

"Err, well, uhh, I mean the danger of being at the bottom of the ocean," he says, nodding vigorously. "I didn't mean anything by that."

You want to argue more, but the chess board flickers and warps. Suddenly it's a completely different configuration, with different pieces.

There's no Queen this time. Instead, the piece representing your Knight flashes three times.

"I guess we have to move the knight."

Okay, let's do this again.

Move the white Knight to spot **A** *ON PAGE 18*
Move the white Knight to spot **B** *ON PAGE 28*
Move the white Knight to spot **C** *ON PAGE 38*

54

You wish you could cautiously descend, but there's no time. With a frightened yelp you leap from the peak.

The smooth face isn't very smooth now that you're plummeting down it: every rock and protruding edge scrapes along your legs and back. You think you can hear Craig yelling behind you, but it's tough to be certain with the air rushing past your ears.

Abruptly, the face ends. You fly into open air, falling the final twenty feet before slamming into the ground.

"Oof!"

Craig lands on your legs, sending bolts of pain up your ankle. You cover your head and lay there until the tremors subside.

"Is it over?" Craig says.

You push to your feet and nearly fall back down as your ankle buckles underneath you. Carefully, you test it again. You'll have a limp, but it should bear your weight.

"I think so. And it looks like the door to the next dome is open."

After all of this, you're not sure you even want to continue. Craig's hesitation seems to match your own.

"I wonder if a whale is what damaged Dome Three," he says.

It's a good hypothesis. You squint out the glass and can barely see Dome Three in the distance, muddled by all the water in between. You try to picture what the dome looked like from the outside.

"Might as well get it over with," you say, more to convince yourself than him. You stride forward with purposeful steps.

Enter Dome Three *ON PAGE 130*

You leap through the air like a circus performer, and for a few brief moments you're a helpless captive of gravity. You watch the next mountain rise up beneath you. It doesn't look like you're going to make it!

You reach out just as you slam into the side, arms scraping along the flat peak. You slide a few inches and become still.

Craig lands next to you, similarly barely holding on. You climb up to the peak and help him up. "That was close."

"I've never jumped that far." Craig glances back the way you came. It looks longer than it felt!

A thought occurs to you. "Hey, so I have a question. If this is a research habitat..."

"Uh huh," Craig says.

"...then where are the living quarters? All we've seen are these big domes. There aren't any beds, or a kitchen, or anything else. Do the researchers live up on the surface, in the research vessel? And only make periodic trips down here?"

"I suspect there are living quarters somewhere in this habitat," Craig says carefully. "But we don't know for sure."

"How do you not know if there are living quarters? You almost sound like you *found* this place..."

Craig interrupts you to point at the next stone slab. "Hey, it's glowing! I think we have our next test..."

Approach the stone structure *ON PAGE 70*

56

"My alma mater's mascot was a marlin," Craig says. "We had a statue like this on the campus lawn. Man, that was such a long time ago..."

The fish is almost vertical, similar to the dolphin one you saw earlier. It looks like it was frozen in mid-leap.

"Their meat is delicious," you say. "If it's fresh. The same day it was caught."

Craig makes a funny face. "It's not against your, like, profession to eat a swordfish? They don't look down on you for that?"

You chuckle. "I'm an oceanographer, not a vegetarian. You can both study them *and* eat them. If anything, it gives me a greater appreciation of the animals."

"If you say so."

To the north is a snake carving above a hall.

To the east is a doorway with a killer whale carving.

To the south is an opening with a hammerhead shark carving.

Craig rubs his stomach. "I wish I had brought some food with us. I didn't expect to leave the boat..."

Go north by *FLIPPING TO PAGE 75*
To go east, *WALK TO PAGE 48*
Or, head south *ON PAGE 64*

"There's a trick to this," Craig mutters. "It's a *riddle*."

You smile. "It sure is. It said *Mary's* mother has four children. Mary is the fourth child!"

Craig's eyes widen.

"The answer is Mary," you announce.

Just as before there's a ringing sound you assume to be positive. Craig bobs his head up and down, and the two of you climb out of the pit to the dome floor. Lights guide you to the third and final pit.

It's just like the first two, empty and featureless. You wait for the voice, which fills your ears and mind.

> *"There are five gears connected in a row,*
> *The first gear connected to the second, the second to the third, and so on.*
> *If you twist the first gear **clockwise**, what direction will the fifth gear rotate?"*

The voice seems strangely excited. Or maybe it's your imagination. It is the final pit in Dome Two, after all.

Craig's staring off in concentration, pointing in the air to try to visualize the puzzle.

Do you know which way the fifth gear would rotate?

If you think it's **clockwise**, *GO TO PAGE 164*
To guess **counter-clockwise**, *TURN TO PAGE 171*

58

The subs keep drifting back and forth as they fall through the water. You focus, waiting for the perfect time to extend the dock. The scientists in the other sub, waving and calling for help, doesn't make it any easier.

You jerk the joystick forward. The docking mechanism connects with a dull *THUD*.

"Did you do it?" Craig asks.

"I... I think so."

"No time for diagnostics," the driver says. "Open the hatch!"

You grab the metal wheel. It hardly moves. You throw all your might into turning it. Slowly it begins to move.

"Be ready to hand them the sealant gel," the driver says. "As soon as they have it we'll need to disconnect and–"

There's a horrifying hissing sound. Before you can stop it, the hatch comes crashing open with the weight of the pacific ocean.

You fly backwards as water pours over you. It must not have been a perfect connection! Craig is scrambling to get out of his harness, but where does he think he'll go? The driver is yelling something, but you can't hear him over the roar of flooding water.

You've screwed it up.

The sub hasn't dived very far. Maybe you'll be able to swim out the hatch and reach the surface. But whether you make it out or not, you won't be visiting the undersea laboratory any time soon, which means this is...

THE END

"I'm an oceanographer, not a physicist or mathematician. Why was I brought here? What's the *point* of all this?"

"You weren't the only one we brought," Craig explains. "We've brought geologists, astrophysicists. We've had the smartest minds in the world trying to figure it all out."

"Figure all of *what* out? Why won't you tell me?"

"It's classified. All we can tell you is–"

Upset with Craig's half-answers, you shove the stone tablet.

Hard.

The entire thing rocks back, rocks forward, and then leans back. In slow motion it falls off the edge of the mountain, crashing down its side and exploding into a thousand crumbling pieces.

When the dust settles, you give Craig a triumphant smile. But he's not looking at you. He's glancing all around, as if waiting for something else.

The soothing robotic voice returns, with a note of curiosity in its tone.

"Subject aggression noted. Unexpected result. More data required. Proceed to Dome Three."

"Huh," Craig says.

"The only way to win is to not play the game," you say.

Craig blinks. "That sounds familiar."

"It's from my favorite movie." You nod toward the other side of the dome, far below you, where the door marked DOME THREE is. "You heard the voice. Let's proceed to Dome Three. That's where we're supposed to be going in the first place, right?"

"Yeah."

You climb down the mountain, carefully avoiding the debris from the destroyed tablet.

You've made it! Enter Dome Three *ON PAGE 130*

60

"Come on!"

You leap to the right, landing ten feet below on the first flat surface. You wobble on the edge, flailing with your hands, but manage to regain your balance. Craig lands next to you a moment later.

The next step is closer, and you carefully jump down to it. The third one is even easier, so you put one hand on the ground and swing yourself down to it. Your feet hit the rock...

...and crash through it as if it's paper.

"Ahh!"

You plummet into darkness, down into the center of the mountain. You hit the ground, sending pain flaring in your ribs. Small pebbles and bits of rock fall over you, and then you hear Craig's weight land somewhere nearby.

From inside the mountain, the quaking is deafening. All you can do is cover your head and hope for the best.

The rumbling stops sometime later. You tentatively open one eye, then the other. They're adjusted to the darkness by now. You're in a small pocket of air, as large as the inside of a car. Rocks wedged together form a ceiling. You're lucky to be alive!

Craig groans and pushes to his feet, hitting his head on the rock ceiling. He groans some more and sits down, holding his head.

"I don't understand why there was a whale so deep," you say.

Craig looks at you like you're nuts. "We're trapped down here, and you're worried about the *whale?*"

"Whales are mammals. They need to surface to breathe. They're known to dive deep at times, but this is farther than any scientist has ever recorded..."

You have a lot of time to think about it. Eventually you'll be rescued by one of the other scientist teams, but you're certainly not proceeding any farther. And what about the symbol on your heads? Those are all questions for next time, a time when you are not stuck at...

THE END

"Mookie's in front of Dustin, and Dustin is ahead of everyone else," you work out. Saying out loud makes you certain. "Mookie is at the front of the line!"

The response is immediate and definitive. A pleasant sounding *DING* cuts the air. You look around the dome to see which of the other two stations lights up, but instead the voice returns:

"Six in a line, six they do meander: David, Dustin, Hanley, Jackie, Mookie, and Xander.

Hanley is behind David and Mookie.
Mookie is in front of Dustin.
Jackie is behind Hanley, Xander and Dustin.
Dustin is in front of Jackie and Xander.
Xander is in front of Hanley and David.
Xander is behind Mookie.

"Wait!' you cry. "We just completed this puzzle."

"Maybe we got it wrong..."

Then the voice adds:

"It's a different question this time: who is at the BACK of the line?"

"Ohh." Craig blinks.

"I guess we should be more patient." You take a deep breath. "Well at least we know it's not Mookie."

Who is in the back of the line?

If it's **David,** *GO TO PAGE 21*
If it's **Dustin,** *GO TO PAGE 31*
If it's **Hanley,** *GO TO PAGE 41*
If it's **Jackie,** *GO TO PAGE 11*
If it's **Xander,** *GO TO PAGE 71*

62

There's laughter of relief on the speaker. "Sub two, that did the trick! Or at least, it's holding the seal well enough to get the buoyancy working. We're going to head back to the surface for repairs. Thanks for the assist."

"Glad to hear it." The driver turns back to you. "Alright. Resuming descent."

You slump back into one of the seats. "All the dangers of the ocean, sharks and bacteria and every kind of poisonous jellyfish, and it's always the mechanical problems that scare me the most."

Craig's face goes blank. "Yeah. If that *was* a mechanical problem."

You're about to ask what he means when the driver cuts in. "Oh wow. That was fast. Didn't realize how far we went while helping the other sub. The research habitat is coming into view now."

You walk the two steps to the front of the submarine. There's a dim light in the distance. "I never get tired of this sight," Craig says.

Slowly, the water becomes clear enough for you to see. And as you do, your breath catches in your throat.

"Oh my gosh..."

The domes are breathtaking. Like tiny little bubbles housing cities of light! You try to imagine how they were constructed. It must have taken years, and billions of dollars.

What have you gotten yourself into?

As your awe fades away, you realize something. "I thought there were *five* domes."

Craig nods. "There are. Or at least, there *were.*"

Find out what he means *ON PAGE 66*

Craig wanders over to one of the computer screens while you go to the map.

It's unlike any map you've ever seen, though it's strangely familiar. It's covered in dots, some larger than others. One of them is as big as a nickel. They glow faintly, each of them individual, like a thousand different Christmas lights.

Lines connect some of the dots, and there's one dot in the center of the map with dozens of lines originating from it. The whole thing is like some half-finished game of connect-the-dots.

You begin to turn away when something catches your eye. You stare at it for five long seconds.

"That's Orion," you mutter. Which makes the whole thing a *star* map. "Why would..."

You cut off as Craig gasps. "I can't believe it," he says from across the room. He's looking at a computer screen. "I just can't! I know Frank speculated, but I never would have believed..."

Better find out what he's looking at. *HEAD TO PAGE 177*

64

The hammerhead shark sculpture stops you in your tracks. Its eyes shine like black glass on the end of its wing-like head. The mouth underneath is a dark cave of jagged teeth.

You open your mouth to tell Craig about how the shark evolved its iconic head shape when he speaks first.

"We're on the outer part of this dome. The west side. See the curving wall?"

You see what he means: the edge of the dome rises up above you, just on the other side of the wall to your left. "Huh. I guess so."

Craig walks to the east wall, where the outline of a door can be seen. But, unlike the other doors, this one is closed. "There's a pentagon-shaped hole here. I think it's for a key."

You throw your hands in the air in exasperation. "Why are there locked doors down here? What kind of a research habitat is this? What are we testing?"

Craig lets out a long breath and says, "I wish I knew."

To the north is a door with a swordfish carved into the wall.

To the east is the locked door–a stingray statue looms over that one, flat and silent.

To the south is a doorway with a moray eel carving.

To go north, *FLIP TO PAGE 56*
If you have the key, go east by *TURNING TO PAGE 72*
Or, go south *TO PAGE 79*

This room holds a statue of a cat. Even in stone, the animal manages to look bored and uncaring.

"I'm more of a dog person," you say.

"I've got a goldfish. I sort of feel like him, now. You know, down in these domes."

To the north is a door with a dolphin carving.

To the east is a door with a ferret or weasel carved over the top.

The wall to the south is blank, though for a split second you thought you saw the outline of a door. Weird.

To go north, *JUMP TO PAGE 32*
Or, go east by *FLIPPING TO PAGE 39*

66

Craig nods at the window. "You can see Dome Three if you squint. It's there, but it has lost all power and has flooded. We're not sure why. That's why you're here"

You unfocus your eyes, and the outline of the dome appears. It looks like it's damaged, somehow.

Before you can ask more, the driver speaks up. "Craig? They're on the radio."

He goes to the front of the submarine and begins speaking into the headset. You press your face to the porthole glass, watching the mysterious underwater habitat grow larger.

The sub maneuvers into the center of the dome ring, where a special dock waits. Everything shakes as it latches on and creates the seal. Craig opens the hatch and you follow him into the dock.

The first thing you notice are the people waiting inside. They're standing in a cluster, arms crossed and with fearful looks on their faces. One man's lab coat is scorched on the side. A woman in a "United States Department of Astrophysics" shirt looks like she's been in a fight: her hair is frazzled and sticking out on one side. Another man whimpers quietly.

The astrophysicist woman jabs a finger into Craig's chest. "I didn't sign up for this," she says. "You didn't warn us!"

"Eleanor, please," Craig begins, but she shoves past him and goes inside the submarine. The others quickly follow.

"You will be debriefed on the surface," Craig says, but the hatch has closed and the sub is already moving. After a moment, he says, "Wait! You're forgetting me!"

He grabs the hatch wheel and tries turning it, but a warning light beeps on the wall, warning him that there's only ocean on the other side.

"What was that all about?" you ask. "I get the feeling that we're going in the wrong direction."

Craig sighs and faces you. He puts on a meager smile. "Everything is fine. I suppose I'll just wait here for the sub to return." He pauses. "Or, I suppose I can go with you. If the excitement is worth it..."

You put your hands on your hips. "Worth what? Go *where*?"

He points. "Into the domes, of course."

You look to where he's pointing. There are five doors, each with a label stamped into the frame: **DOME ONE, DOME TWO,** all the way to **DOME FIVE.**

"If you imagine the laboratory is a big wheel," Craig says, "then we're at the center. Hallways connect to each dome, like spokes."

"Yes, but what are in the domes? What oceanography experiments will I be performing? You still haven't explained anything. I need to know why I'm here!"

Craig takes a long look at you before responding. He removes his tie and drops it on the floor. You get the feeling he's deciding just how much to tell you.

"We need to get to Dome Three, so you can figure out why it flooded. I'll know how to proceed from there." He says no more.

You cross your arms. "I don't know why you're intentionally leaving details out, but I'm not going any further until you give me some straight answers."

Craig smiles apologetically. "Actually, the contract you signed states that–"

"Okay, *fine*," you say. "Enough about what I signed ten years ago. Let's get this over with."

He nods as if he expected nothing less. "It will make more sense as we proceed, I hope. Now. Which dome should we begin with? It looks like some of the tunnels are damaged..."

You take a closer look at the five doors. There's a light next to each one: **DOME ONE** and **DOME FIVE** are green, but the others are red.

"The tunnels to Dome One and Dome Five are the only ones operational? But Dome Three is on the opposite side of the ring!"

"There are individual tunnels connecting each dome to its adjacent one," Craig explains. "So we have two paths we can take: Dome One, to Dome Two, to Dome Three. Or Dome Five, to Dome Four, to Dome Three."

"And you don't know which way is better?"

He shrugs. "Usually I stay in the submarine. I'm just an administrator. I've never been inside before!"

Which way will it be?

To begin in Dome One, *TURN TO PAGE 110*
Or, give Dome Five a try *ON PAGE 150*

68

"What kind of a quiz is this? This is easy!"

"Wait a second," Craig says.

But it's obvious to you. So obvious, in fact, that you blurt out what is very clearly the answer: "Her name is July. April, May, June, and *July*."

Craig smacks his forehead. "No! Wait, I... aww, Jessica! I had the right answer!"

"Well then what was it?"

He never has a chance to respond. There's a hissing sound in the walls, and the robotic voice suddenly says:

"Incorrect. Freezing specimens for later examination and classification."

"Wait, freezing us for *what?*"

"Forget that," Craig says, "the freezing part is what worries me!"

The hissing in the walls turns out to be dozens of nozzles. They spray you from all sides at once, coating you in a sticky foam substance. You try wiping it from your face, but even before your hand reaches your head it turns numb. You hold it there halfway in the air, unable to move.

Your entire body is frozen!

When the foam fully hardens, you can still breathe and see. But you're paralyzed as the pit shifts and detaches, and you have the sensation that it's being moved through the air. You've forgotten that you're at the bottom of the ocean. Massive pincers appear above you, gripping the foam interior of the pit, which is now shaped like a traffic cone. It pulls the entire cone out of the pit, giving you a view of an enormous warehouse-like room.

The pincers swing you through the air, placing you on some sort of shelf. Out of the corner of your eye–you can't be certain, since you can't move your head!– you see a long row of similar translucent cones.

And it looks like there are others inside them. Other *people.*

You try to scream, but no noise comes out. You wish you could turn and see Craig, find out what's really going on here. How could you have gone down there without getting some real answers? You would definitely do things differently if you could, but that will have to be another time, since you're frozen at...

THE END

"That's a Portuguese Man-Of-War," you tell Craig as you walk through the doorway. "It's one of the most venomous creatures on the planet."

Craig shivers. "I hate jellyfish."

You grin. "*Technically*, it's not a jellyfish. It's a siphonophore. That's a common mistake."

"Don't care, still hate it."

You go on as if he hadn't interrupted you. "The tentacles can paralyze small fish and other prey, even when detached. The toxins can be deadly to humans, if no treatment is..."

You trail off as you enter the room. There's no statue in this room, just a writhing mass of slime on the ground. These are *real* Portuguese Man-Of-Wars!

"Okay, don't panic," you say, ignoring the craziness of the situation. "Just keep our distance. They're not in water, so we can easily–"

You cut off as one of them whips around like a lawnmower blade. A long, bluish tentacle rolls across the floor and slaps you in the ankle.

"Ahhh!"

You fall backwards into the wall, clutching your leg. It feels like fire is running underneath your skin! You've been stung dozens of times by venomous creatures, but for some reason this hurts worse than you ever remember.

"I'll be fine, I'm not allergic," you say. "But we need to get back to the surface just to be safe. Sometimes, in extreme cases..."

Craig's shaking his head. "The door closed behind us!"

You realize he's right: the door you entered is gone, replaced by the spongy black material of the wall. There's another exit, but it's across the room.

On the other side of all the not-jellyfish.

Maybe you'll be able to hold out until they stop moving. Those types of creatures aren't *supposed* to survive outside water for very long. In the mean time you're in too much pain to continue, so this is...

THE END

70

The third–and final–peak in Dome Three also has a massive stone slab on it, although this one is three-sided, like a triangle-shaped rod sticking out of the ground. The first side faces you. There's a carving of some sphere, like a marble, with words underneath:

WHAT POSITION ORBITS THE LARGEST PLANET IN YOUR SOLAR SYSTEM?

"Ohh, that sphere carved into the rock is a planet," Craig says.

He's right. "It's Jupiter," you say. "The largest planet in the solar system. But what does it mean by position?"

"I think it's asking which number it is from the sun. If it's the first planet, second, etc."

"Okay. So earth is the third planet from the sun, obviously."

But do you know which Jupiter is?

If the answer is fourth, *TURN TO PAGE 119*
To guess fifth, *BLAST TO PAGE 146*
Or if you think it's sixth, *ROTATE TO PAGE 135*

"Got any good guesses?" you ask Craig.

He's scrunching his face, staring off into nothing. "If Mookie is... and David is..."

"I don't suppose there's a time limit, is there?" you ask nobody in particular.

"Xander," Craig says. "Xander is our answer!"

He sounds awfully confident, which fills you with hope. But it only lasts a moment as the robotic voice replies:

"INCORRECT. Subject: failure. Proceed to next dome."

Craig reacts like someone hit him in the chest with a hammer. "Aww. I thought for sure... I guess I'm no good at these sorts of things. I should stay in the office."

You put a reassuring arm around his shoulder. "Nonsense. I didn't know it either." You glance across the room. "Besides, the door to Dome Three opened! So we're still getting to where we need to go."

But that doesn't make him feel any better, at least not that you can tell.

You lead him into the tunnel to Dome Three.

Cheer up and *ADVANCE TO PAGE 130*

72

"Glad we found this key earlier," you say. It fits into the keyhole perfectly.

A seam forms in the wall, and it parts like a curtain despite being solid. There's a long hallway ahead.

The hall opens into the stingray room. As expected, there's a stingray statue on a pedestal in the center of the room.

You're getting impatient, so you quickly scan the room.

To the east is a door with a barracuda carved into the wall.

To the west is the door with the hammerhead shark.

To go east, *FLIP TO PAGE 80*
Or, head back by *GOING TO PAGE 64*

It feels awfully crowded in the sub—you're crammed elbow to elbow. There are a lot of red lights flashing in the cockpit, and the driver is too focused to say anything.

Everyone is looking to you.

You jump out of your seat. "Let's get out of here."

One of the other scientists helps you crank the wheel on the hatch. It moves a finger-length, then another, then it's spinning so fast that—

SWOOSH.

Water gushes inside, throwing you back against your seat. It's like a fire hose, so strong that even with your eyelids closed it stings your eyes. Within seconds the entire submarine is flooded.

You pull yourself through the hatch, and then you're in open sea. There's a whole lot of *nothing* in every direction. You kick, thrusting yourself up toward the distant surface, exhaling the entire time so your lungs don't expand as the pressure diminishes. It's an emergency ascent, and you've done it a million times. Hopefully the others know what to do.

You burst into open air just before passing out. The salty air tastes sweeter than you could ever imagine. One by one the other scientists appear all around you, bobbing on the surface. You wave to the research vessel, a few hundred feet to your left.

Eventually they'll send small craft to scoop you out of the water, but you've missed your chance. One submarine crashed, and the other stays down there for a long time. Part of you is relieved. You'll be able to get back to school and catch up on papers that need grading. But another part of you feels a deep sense of regret at having reached...

THE END

74

You throw yourself on the ground just as the Bishop shoots a beam of light from the tip of his staff. The beam sizzles through the air, making your hair stand up for a moment, but it misses you and hits the far wall.

"Come on!"

You jump to your feet and follow Craig's voice. He's already across the room, at the door marked DOME FOUR. It's wide open!

Zig-zagging to avoid more shots from the Bishops, you reach Craig. The two of you fall into the dark tunnel, and the door closes shut with a muted *THWACK*.

You're breathing hard. "What on earth was *that*?"

Craig sucks in air. His face is red. "I don't know. But it sure was exciting!"

You roll your eyes.

Head into Dome Four *ON PAGE 140*

The statue in the next room looks like a coil of rope you'd find on a pier. The snake's head is in the center, surrounded by rings of its body. Even though it's made of that black spongy material, it gives you the creeps.

For some reason, you have the sudden impulse to touch it. You reach out with tentative fingers, curious as to what will happen if...

Craig grabs your wrist when you're inches away. "Don't."

"Why not?"

"I don't know. I just have a bad feeling about these statues, okay?"

You pull your hand back and give him an even stare. "Why? What's the point of these statues, anyways? And the maze? Huh?"

"I told you, I don't know. Nobody does."

Annoyed by his avoidance of the question, you impulsively dart toward the statue. You touch the carving and immediately flinch as if it will come to life.

But nothing happens. It's just a statue.

"Hey," you say. "There's something behind it." You reach around the statue...

...and come up with a small, metal object. The object has a short handle, with an end shaped like a three-dimensional pentagon. Grooves are set into each side's face in random configurations. It almost looks like a futuristic...

"Key!" Craig says. "That's a key! I remember seeing photos of that, from of the previous attempts."

"Attempts?"

Craig blinks, then scratches his head. "*Tests.* I meant tests."

You roll your eyes. "Well, it's a dead end. We have to go back."

You've found the pentagon shaped key! You might need it later.

Return to the Swordfish room *ON PAGE 56*

76

You turn the cable around and shove it into the left outlet. You know it should fit, but something is keeping it from going in all way. You grip it with both hands and lean into it, putting all your weight behind–

BZZZZZZTTTTTTT!

There's a flash of light and a crashing sound in your ears. For a long moment nothing happens.

Slowly, your vision returns. You're on your back, staring up at the dome ceiling. Your head hurts. And your neck. As a matter of fact, *everything* aches, from your chest all the way down to your heels.

You groan. "What happened..."

Craig appears over you. He looks terrified. "It's okay. You shocked yourself." He looks around. "I'm, uhh, going to get help. Yes! That's why I'm going to do. Find some help for you."

He disappears. You can hear him muttering to himself as he goes: "Should have stayed in my office where I belong. Too much excitement. Don't know what I was thinking..."

Hopefully he'll find help. You don't seem to be critically injured, although you're too weary to move. Maybe next time you won't shock yourself plugging in a cable as thick as an elephant trunk, but this time you *did*, which means that this is...

THE END

"The entrance didn't have a carving above the door," you reason out. "So maybe the exit is the same way. Let's go that way."

You confidently stride into the hallway. It's tough to tell, but based on the dome above you *think* you're where you expect the exit to be. If there is one.

Unlike the other parts of the maze, this hallway isn't straight. It twists and turns, left and right and even doubling back on itself. It has to be the way out. It has to be! Your excitement builds, to the point where you're practically jogging when it opens up into a room.

You stop in your tracks. For a moment you don't understand. There's a dolphin statue on the far doorway, and an urchin one to your right. That seems weirdly familiar...

"*What?*" Craig blurts out. "This is the entrance! We're back at the beginning!"

Oh no. You realize he's right.

You spin around to retrace your steps through the twisting tunnel, but it's not there anymore. There's only the smooth wall, with no sign that any hallway ever existed.

"Well that's funny," is all you can say.

Looks like you're back to square one. *TURN TO PAGE 128*

78

You moved the Knight last time, and it worked out well. You pick it up again, think for a moment, and then place it on the board.

For three long seconds, nothing happens. Then the same voice speaks inside your mind again, and this time it seems disappointed:

"Test failure. Proceed to Dome Four for next test."

The chess board flashes red, then disappears entirely. You and Craig are alone in the circle—which is also now red like the others, instead of green. And the door marked DOME FOUR is now wide open. You never even heard the door move.

"I don't understand why we get to continue if we failed the test," you say. "That doesn't make *any* sense."

Craig smiles awkwardly. "Yeah. Well. Let's just take it for what it is and move on, shall we?"

You want to demand more answers from him, but you're beginning to suspect he knows as little as you. Rolling your eyes, you move toward the door.

Check out Dome Four *ON PAGE 140*

The statue in the middle of this room is made up of dozens of moray eels, a tangled mess of spotted scales and eyes and teeth. Real eels never bothered you, but these give you the creeps, so you give the statue a wide berth.

To the north is a doorway with a hammerhead shark.

To the east is a jellyfish carving above the doorway. There's a trail of something wet heading that way.

To the south is a blank door without any sort of statue.

"Wonder where that one goes," Craig says. "Maybe it's the exit?"

If you want to head north, *GO TO PAGE 64*
You can go east by *TURNING TO PAGE 69*
Or, you can walk south by *SLIDING BACK TO PAGE 77*

80

Barracudas are your least favorite fish, and you've seen a *lot* of fish. The way their narrow face seems to follow you around while scuba diving always unnerved you.

Thankfully, this statue doesn't do that. You pass by it, admiring the craftsmanship of the sculpture. It was expertly done.

"What's up with this room?" Craig says.

You realize what he means: each doorway is blank. There's no carving or anything to indicate where they lead.

"Huh."

There are four ways to go: north, south, east, or west.

"West was the room with the stingray," you say. "So we know that's not the right way. Unless we want to go backwards."

Craig shrugs. "The maze entrance was also blank. Maybe this is a good sign? That we're near the exit?"

You glance up at the dome ceiling high above. You wish it held some clue as to which way to go.

To go north, *FLIP TO PAGE 65*
To go south, *TURN TO PAGE 88*
To go east, *GO TO PAGE 37*
To go west, *RUN TO PAGE 72*

With the timer beeping down, and the immense emptiness of the dome, you feel nervous. Sweat beads at your temples. You're an oceanographer, not a bomb defuser!

Hoping you're right, you snip the sixth wire. You flinch, waiting for the explosion.

One breath. Two. The explosion never comes.

"I... I think it worked," Craig says. He adjusts his glasses. "I think it worked!"

The computerized voice sounds different this time. It's almost... *pleased.*

"Subject: passed. Proficient in strategy and spacial reasoning."

A cylinder the size of a AAA battery emerges from the side of the box. You realize what it looks like–a laser pointer–right before the blue beam hisses toward you. It splits in mid-air, hitting both you and Craig in the foreheads.

You cringe, expecting there to be white-hot pain, but all you feel is a tingling on your skin. The laser cuts off.

Craig rubs his forehead. "What was that all about?" You realize there's a symbol now glowing on his skin, no larger than a thumbprint:

After you describe it to Craig, he nods. "You've got it too."

You rub your own forehead unconsciously. "What does it mean?"

"I don't know. But we passed the test." He points. "And the door to Dome Four is open."

Nice job, I guess? *HEAD TO PAGE 140*

82

The Raven room has a statue of the namesake bird, and due to its color it even looks normal.

What's *not* normal, however, is the way the statue is floating in the air. You approach it, circling all around.

Craig waves his hand underneath the bird, then over the top. "No strings holding it in place."

"Weird..." you say. You brush it off as another mystery of the underwater habitat.

To the north is a door with a hawk carving.

To the south is a door with an ostrich carved above the door.

"Did you hear that?" Craig snaps.

"What?"

He cocks his head, listening. "I thought I heard something that way." He gestures to the south. "Maybe not."

But, while pointing in that direction, you notice something scratched into the wall. It looks like chalk, white against the black material.

The way to be free
lies with eights, or the sea

"What does that mean? I don't want to have to swim to get out of here..."

"I don't know," you say. "And more importantly, who wrote it?" You decide it's best to just move on.

If you want to head to the hawk room, *TURN TO PAGE 27*
To enter the ostrich room, *GO TO PAGE 36*

You dodged once and it seemed to work well. So there's no reason to do anything different this time.

The glow at the end of the wizard's staff intensifies. It makes the air hum with electricity. You bend your knees, and just before you think it's going to fire you throw yourself to the side, rolling across the platform.

Your timing is perfect–you jump just as a thick bolt of energy shoots from the staff. But instead of moving in a straight line, the bolt begins to change directions! You watch in horror as it turns in the air like a curveball. Despite your roll it grazes your arm, sending your sword clattering to the ground.

The wizard looks down at you with boredom. You get the impression he was hoping for a better challenge than that.

Abruptly, the hologram disappears: the wizard, his horse, your sword and shield. Everything is gone in the blink of an eye as the screens turn off. Then there's a voice, which seems to come from everywhere and nowhere all at once, like it's speaking in your imagination:

"Subject: failure. Proceed to next dome."

The screens go blank. Across the room, the door to Dome Two suddenly opens.

"Did... did you hear that?" Craig says.

"Of course I did. I think it came from the speakers." You get to your feet. "It said I failed, but we get to go to the next dome anyways. What's up with that?"

Craig looks uncomfortable. "I don't know. Let's just go."

At least it was just a hologram. Proceed to Dome Two *ON PAGE 120*

84

"Io is the most volcanic moon, because it orbits so close to Jupiter itself. That causes tidal heating!"

For a long while there's no answer. Everything seems very still, except the fish swimming on the other side of the dome glass.

Then the carved words on the slab begin to swirl, twist, morph. It's as if they're made of sand, and someone is running their fingers through them. Eventually the words are gone, replaced by a perfect circle the size of a quarter.

From which a blue laser shoots.

It strikes you in the forehead, hissing like a frying pan. You open your mouth to cry out but are too scared to move or make a sound. Eventually the laser stops, then does the same to Craig.

When it ends, the stone slab descends into the ground, disappearing with a final hollow *KONG*.

You turn to Craig. There's a symbol on his forehead, glowing slightly:

You describe it to him, and he nods. "You've got the same thing."

You touch your forehead. It *feels* smooth, as if nothing had happened. It doesn't even hurt.

"Looks like the door to Dome Three is open!"

You see that Craig is right. You take a deep breath and let it out. "Okay. Let's climb down and–"

Suddenly the entire mountain begins to rumble.

You look up at the dome ceiling. A dark shape approaches, growing larger every second. You realize what it is just before it hits.

"That's a whale!"

You're thrown to the ground as the whale slams into the dome. Craig falls too, and nearly slips over the edge, but you grab his arm and pull him back. Above, the whale is swimming away.

You get to your feet. Everything is still shaking, reverberating like an endless music note. Rocks tumble down the side of the mountain, and cracks form in the side. It's all falling apart!

"We need to get down from here *now.*"

Craig's head tilts up and down in a big nod.

You examine the mountainside. It appears far steeper than it did before! There's a stepped path straight down, but before you can move half of the steps slough away. The rocks fall through the air and shatter into a thousand pieces on the dome floor.

You're running out of time. There's a smooth face to the left you can slide down. On the right, there are more rocky faces you could step along. If they don't fall away, that is.

Which way do you go? Roll a die! (if you don't have one, pick a random number from 1 to 6)

If you roll a 1, 3, 4, or 6, *SLIDE TO PAGE 54*
If you roll a 2 or 5, *HOP TO PAGE 60*

86

You jam the cable into the middle outlet. It's heavy, and doesn't fit easily. Probably because it's so big–it's like an elephant trunk! You push harder, waiting for the satisfying click that will verify–

BAAZZZZZITTTTTTT!

All the lights in the dome begin to flicker. You jerk your hand away from the plug as if it's a snake. There's a humming sound in the floor and air, like a thousand bumblebees swirling all around you. Craig moans, darting his head each way.

Suddenly you're engulfed in darkness. For a few moments you see the after-image of the dome lights, triangle frames that appear white whenever you blink your eyes. Aside from that, the only thing you can see is the green light at the door to Dome Two.

"I think I broke it."

Craig lets out a nervous laugh. "Yeah. But hey–I think the door is open now."

The green light outlines the doorframe, and you realize he's right. Thankful that the room was mostly empty, devoid of things to trip over, you make your way over there. The tunnel stands open, waiting.

"Well we're moving on. That has to be good, right?"

"Sure," Craig says, but he sounds anything but certain.

Head to Dome Two by *LIMPING TO PAGE 120*

Thinking fast, you run to the locker. The door swings open and you're greeted by the best possible sight: underwater suits with glass helmets, all hanging from hooks.

You grab the first two suits, tossing one to Craig. He stares at it like he doesn't understand.

"Hurry!" you say, stepping into the feet of your suit.

Already the water is at your ankles and rising fast. The door into the room is gone–all you see are walls. Good thing you didn't go that way. At any moment the glass could completely give way. Your fingers fumble over the elastic fabric as you pull it up your legs.

"It's too big," Craig says.

"It doesn't matter! Hurry!"

There's no zipper; the material just sort of folds together seamlessly. Somehow it holds the water at bay, though, so you pull it up over your body and stick your arms through the holes. The glass helmet goes over your head, and a soft suction sound tells you it's sealed. Craig was right: the suits are way too big. It's like they were made for 7-foot-tall basketball players, with bunches of the fabric hanging loosely around your waist. But hey, it's good enough to keep from drowning.

Craig is still struggling, so you quickly help him finish dressing. By the time his helmet falls into place the water is at your waist. Moments later, the glass wall finally gives way. Within seconds the dome is completely flooded from floor to ceiling.

"Whew," Craig says. You can hear him clearly, so there must be some sort of radio in the helmet. "Nice thinking, Jessica."

You spend only a moment reveling in the victory. You may be alive, but you're still trapped underwater! There's an SUV-sized hole in the wall where the glass gave way. You can see the murky ocean beyond.

"I guess it's time to go for a walk."

"I don't see any other option," Craig agrees.

Taking care to avoid the glass shards sticking up from the ground, you step through the hole and onto the ocean floor. The boots of the suit sink into the sandy bottom a couple of millimeters, a harsh reminder that you're leaving safety.

You decide it's best to stick close to the dome wall. But which way should you go?

To go left, *TURN TO PAGE 190*
To go right, *FLIP TO PAGE 169*

88

This room has no statue. Worse, it ends at the edge of the glass dome.

You sigh. "A dead end."

"No, look!"

There's a computer screen in the wall, as dark as the ocean beyond. You approach, and when you get within reach you're suddenly frozen in place as if held by imaginary rope.

Before you have a chance to panic, a blue beam cuts the air and strikes you in the forehead. You wince as it moves with a soft crackling sound, though there's no pain. It does the same to Craig, and then it's gone and you're free as if nothing happened.

Craig rubs his forehead. You squint at the symbol now there:

"Okay, so we've been marked," Craig says. "Whatever that means. But we're still at a dead end in this maze! How are we supposed to get back?" He pounds the wall in frustration.

As if the research habitat somehow heard him, a deep rumble grows in the ground. Like the machinery of a rollercoaster winding up!

"Craig, what did you do!"

"I don't know." His eyes widen. "I don't know!"

Don't panic. Or at least, try not to. *TURN TO PAGE 182*

None of these scientists know any more than you do. Craig is the one with the answers. The open connection to sub one calls to you.

"Wait!" you say, throwing off your seatbelt and tossing the tube of sealant gel to the geologist. "I'm coming across!"

Before anyone can stop you, you're jumping into the connection tube. The walls are made of a flexible plastic composite, but it bears your weight just fine. 130 pounds of oceanographer is nothing compared to the full weight of the sea pressing on the plastic!

Craig leans back, shocked, but then reaches out to help you through. As soon as you're on your feet he closes the hatch and spins the wheel until it won't tighten any further, then uses a joystick to disengage the connector arm.

"Okay, she's through," the driver of the sub says over the radio. "Go ahead, sub one."

There's an anxious minute of silence on the radio. All you and Craig can do is stand and wait.

Will the sealant work? Or did you save your own skin by jumping subs?

FIND OUT ON PAGE 62

90

You picture a map of Europe in your head. "Poland borders Germany to the east. On the west, it borders the Netherlands, Belgium, and... France!"

Craig nods. "So by process of elimination, Italy is the answer!"

A soft bell rings in the air, seemingly everywhere and nowhere all at once. You examine the floor and ceiling, searching for speakers, but you see none.

The computerized voice calls out another question:

"Brazil, Ecuador, and Australia. Which country does the equator NOT pass through?"

"Oh, this one's easy," Craig says.

Is it easy?

To guess Brazil, *TURN TO PAGE 19*
If Ecuador is correct, *FLIP TO PAGE 105*
Or, if you think Australia is right, *GO TO PAGE 147*

"I'm fairly certain the answer is electron," you say.

The voice responds immediately:

"INCORRECT. Subjects not proficient in subatomic knowledge. Proceed to Dome Three."

Far below, at the edge of the dome, the door slides open.

"Huh," you say. "We got it wrong, but we still get to move on? Seriously, what's the deal with this research habitat, Craig?"

The man has no answer for you. Together, you climb down the mountain and head into the next tunnel. You give one final look back into the dome you were inside for barely five minutes.

Dome Three! Walk inside *TO PAGE 130*

92

"I'm curious as to what will happen when we try Exit Ship," you say. "Maybe a submarine will arrive?"

"Umm," Craig says. He stares off, thinking about it.

His indecision drives you nuts. You've been down there a while. It's time to *do something.* You press the Exit Ship button.

"Subject departure: acceptable. Information download: complete. Returning subjects to previous time and location."

"Returning us *where?*" you say, just as the world goes black.

RETURN TO PAGE 15

A sword isn't very good against an axe. And you're tempted to use your shield to block the blow... but the goblin has an awful lot of momentum. He's practically stumbling as he runs.

You wait until he's nearly upon you before jumping to the side.

It's too late for the goblin to react. He brings the axe head down into empty air with all his might. The motion throws him off balance. He tries to get his feet under him, but he's falling, unable to stop himself.

And while he's falling, you swing your sword sideways across your body. It passes through the goblin's body without resistance–it's a hologram, remember?

But the goblin winces as he falls to the ground. He jumps back up, but slumps his shoulders in defeat. He gives you a grudging nod of respect and then, in the blink of an eye, he's gone.

"Nice move!" Craig says. "Do you fight a lot of goblins as an Oceanographer?"

"I played dodgeball when I was in grade school," you say with a smile. "But that's the closest I've ever come to this."

There's motion on the computer screen in front of you. A figure on a horse comes galloping toward you, dressed in green robes that drape down the side of the animal. A long staff is held in one hand.

"A wizard!" Craig yells.

The wizard pulls the horse to a stop thirty feet from you. He looks like every stereotypical wizard you've ever seen in a movie, with a grey beard and spectacles. He frowns down at you and points his staff in your direction.

The air vibrates, and the staff begins to glow.

Whatever is about to happen, it *can't* be good.

To try dodging the attack, *ROLL TO PAGE 83*
If you want to block with your shield, *GO TO PAGE 134*
To charge the wizard with your sword, *RUN TO PAGE 107*

94

There's not much precedent in your instincts for what to do when faced with an alien. A big alien. Deep down, you're just a mammal, and a scared one at that.

You run.

You can't tell if the alien is following you, or if it's making any noises. The sound of your ragged breathing is all you hear as you sprint through the spaceship, practically sliding around the corners in your desperation to get away. The panic is all you feel, and it drives you forward relentlessly.

Turning a corner, you freeze. Ahead of you, in the middle of the corridor, is another of the tall, slender creatures. Its silhouette is outlined against the deeper lights of the ship, and it does not move.

You whirl back the way you came, pulling Craig along. You get to the next intersection and stop. More of the aliens block each way, all of them staring silently.

"Wh–what–what do we do?" Craig stammers. "Jessica?"

"I don't know," you say.

Something nudges you forward, like an invisible wall. There's nothing behind you, yet you're unable to stop yourself from moving. Telekinesis. The aliens can move things with their mind! Somehow that doesn't even scare you any further.

You allow yourself to be shepherded through the halls. One of the aliens leads the way, walking with long strides while his arms hang loosely at the side. Every time the invisible force pushes you, the alien cocks its head to the side like a dog. You'd be fascinated if you weren't so, you know, *terrified.*

A door opens and you're back in the control room. Three of the aliens stand in the center of the room, unmoving, like statues.

The door closes behind you.

This looks like the end for you and Craig. *TURN TO PAGE 99*

The timer beeps with each second, a constant reminder that you're running out of time.

"I don't know which one to cut."

"Just guess!" Craig says.

You hold the cutters over wire one, then three. Finally you stop at wire five. It feels right.

SNIP.

The explosion sends you flying across the room, where you crash into the glass wall of the dome. For a long while you sit on the ground, groaning.

As you get up you realize you cracked the glass! The cracks begin spreading, spiderwebbing across in all directions. The glass finally breaks with a loud *WHOOSH.*

You run from the water, but the doors to the next dome are closed! You turn around...

...and the hole in the dome is suddenly repaired.

"What... how..." you say.

"I didn't see what happened," Craig says. "How could it do that? It was just broken!"

You have a bigger problem, though. An octopus was swept inside with the water! It's the size of a monster truck, eight tentacles slurping across the floor.

It turns to face you. It takes its first awkward step, then another.

There's nowhere for you to go. You're still in amazement that the dome repaired itself–were you just imagining things?–but your wonder won't last long. As the octopus nears you and Craig this is a very wet version of...

THE END

96

You match up the prongs to the third outlet. Holding the thick cable with both hands, you jam it into place.

There's a soft hum in the air, and a *KA-CHUNK, KA-CHUNK, KA-CHUNK* sound of machinery in the floor.

"Look, it worked!" Craig says. The screens on top of the first platform are lighting up.

Filled with excitement, you jog back up the steps to the platform. You step into the center, so that the three screens surround you on three sides. A wave of vertigo comes over you, but only for a heartbeat. It's so real, it feels like you're there!

"Woah," Craig says.

You look down. Holograms in the floor are projecting an image on your body. You're a knight, covered in plate mail on your legs and chest. You're holding a sword in one hand, and tower shield in the other, polished so shiny that it almost looks like a mirror. You wave them around: even though they look real, they pass through your body harmlessly.

"Is this a videogame?"

"Maybe? I'm not sure. I haven't examined the footage from this dome yet..."

The screens show a grassy plain, with rolling hills in the distance. There's motion on the edge of a hill. A small figure comes running toward you. His skin is green, and he has orange hair as thick as straw. He's about half your size. It's a goblin!

He's also carrying an axe in both hands, with a vicious half-moon blade. He's running faster, raising the axe above his head. In a few seconds he'll reach you–or at least, his *picture* will reach you.

Even though it's not real, you get the feeling you need to do something. That your decision is important.

To use your sword, *SWING TO PAGE 141*
If you want to block with your shield, *GO TO PAGE 116*
To try dodging the goblin, *STEP ASIDE TO PAGE 93*

"We're going to move it diagonally," you say, plucking the Queen between your fingers. You slide her toward the King, dropping her down in the adjacent space with an emphatic click.

But the black player's King begins moving. Realization washes over you as it captures your Queen, negating your move.

"I forgot Kings can move that way," you mumble.

"I thought you were Dean of Stanford."

You round on him. "I'm the Dean of Earth Sciences. That has literally nothing to do with chess!"

"I just thought you'd be smarter, is all. The other scientists..."

You grit your teeth and glance at the board. The entire thing *blinks* for an instant, like a computer screen buffering and then catching up with itself. You realize the board is back to its original configuration.

"I guess we get a second chance," Craig says. "Maybe I should choose this time..."

You step up to the board. You're feeling weirdly competitive all of a sudden. You know you can get checkmate!

To move the Queen vertically, *GO TO PAGE 126*
Or, move the Queen horizontally *ON PAGE 52*

"I... uhh..." Craig stammers. You try to say something but your mouth is completely dry.

An ALIEN! What's the best option here?

To run away, *FLEE TO PAGE 94*
To try communicating, *GO TO PAGE 100*

There's a long, pregnant silence. You're acutely aware that you're surrounded: three aliens before you, and the other two behind. The way they all stare at you reminds you of an animal at the zoo.

One of them cocks its head, and a flow of words echo in your brain.

Preevyeht?

Bonjour?

Language. Yes? It sounds vaguely feminine, almost identical to the computer-like voice you've heard throughout the tests in the research habitat.

"Yes!" you say. "This is the language we speak. English. Hello!"

"Hi," Craig says.

Greetings. Gil-like flaps open on the side of the alien's head. *We are very excited to be here! We did not expect to wake from hibernation until the return.*

"Return?" Craig said.

Yes. This time it's one of the others speaking. You're not sure how you know that, but you do. *This craft is programmed to run automatically. We are a backup crew in case any errors occur. Once the data was collected and the ship was safely back in interstellar space we would be woken to review it and set a new course.*

"Why not review it while here? Why hibernate at all?" you ask.

To avoid tainting the tests. A computer can more objectively gather information on your planet's species.

The way they're talking about earth is oddly disconcerting. "Why have you come here?" you ask. "What is the purpose of these tests? Did we pass?"

The aliens do not answer for several breaths. Your question has disturbed them.

That is not for us to say.

Our purpose here is complex, another says.

This is highly irregular, says one of them behind you. *The results cannot be trusted.*

We must consult the arbiter.

Yes. Immediately.

"Hold on a second," you say. "Why can't the tests be trusted?"

Our presence has tainted them, the alien in the middle says. You get the sense that it's in charge. *It has altered your behavior.*

We must leave and return at a later time, another agrees.

Leave and come back? What does that mean? *GO TO PAGE 151*

100

There's no hope of running, not in a ship from where you cannot escape. Even if the elevator door *hadn't* disappeared.

The alien stands up straight. Its eyes regard you coldly. It reminds you of a bird.

You push down your fear until it becomes a slow simmer in the back of your mind. You have three college degrees. Think!

You hold up your palms in a placating gesture. The alien simply stares. "Hello," you say.

"We come in peace!" Craig blurts out.

You give him a look. *What?* his expression seems to say. That's when you see the symbols on his forehead, and are reminded of why you're down there in the first place.

"Look!" you say, pointing at your own forehead. "We have gone through the domes. We are *humans.*"

The alien remains expressionless. You jump back as it steps past you, loping down the corridor. An invisible barrier pushes you, forcing you to follow it. How is it doing that? You remember a course you took when you were an undergrad, on theoretical physics. Telekinesis was one of the subjects. The ability to move things with your mind.

You shiver, and continue following, because you have no other choice. The fear bubbling down in the pit of your stomach begins to grow.

You allow yourself to be shepherded through the halls. At some point another alien appears behind you, following along.

A door opens. You're back in the control room, except now there are three other aliens standing in the center. They remain perfectly still, like statues.

The door closes.

Hopefully they're vegetarian. *FIND OUT ON PAGE 99*

"Might as well start at the beginning," you say. "Dome One it is."

You approach the door, which is steel and doesn't have any handle or knob. You take a step to examine it closer, and without warning it slides open, disappearing into the wall.

"Fancy."

The tunnel is completely dark, except for strange blue lights recessed into the floor. The walls and ceiling are unlike anything you've ever seen before: they're black like metal, dull instead of shiny. Similar to coal. You touch the surface and discover that it's soft!

"It's a special carbon polymer," Craig says. "Very advanced. It will probably be years before we can make it commercially available..."

"It reminds me of sea sponges," you observe. "Industrial sea sponges."

It takes at least two minutes to reach the end of the hall, where another door waits. Like the first one, it opens automatically, leading into the bright dome.

The sight takes your breath away.

Explore the dome *ON PAGE 110*

102

The timer ticks down. Your pulse grows faster with every second.

With trembling hands, you cut wire four.

SNIP.

Something mechanical clicks inside the bomb. The countdown timer suddenly begins descending three times as fast!

35

32

29

26

23

"Get away!"

You close the lid and run away as fast as you can in a random direction. You're halfway to the wall of the dome when–

KABOOM!

The blast knocks you onto your belly, but thankfully doesn't do anything worse than that. You get back up and, after making sure Craig is okay, look back at the ring.

The pedestal the bomb was on is completely gone, and part of the floor has been ripped open. Sparks fly out of the crevice. The three rings are now powered off, and the door marked DOME FOUR is acting funky.

You approach the door. It's opening and closing randomly, making a loud banging noise. "The computer system must be damaged," you say.

Craig nods.

Feeling like a putt putt golf ball running through a windmill, you jump through the doorway as it opens. Craig follows a moment later.

"At least we got to proceed," you say.

"And we didn't get blown up!"

Time to see what Dome Four has in store *ON PAGE 140*

"Whatever we do, I don't want another one of those *alien* computers scanning me again!" you say to Craig. "We need to find another way out of here."

The wall where the elevator was is now perfectly smooth. You'd hoped it would open automatically for you, but it appears that's just wishful thinking. You look around the room, scanning for any important detail that might help you.

"Maybe if we..." you trail off. "Craig? Craig!"

He's walking toward the red circle, his movements slow and zombie-like. "We have to," he says.

"No. No we don't!"

"We'll never get out if we don't do what they want!"

He's almost to the circle. You can't abandon your friend, even though he's kept secret the true nature of the habitat. You groan as you realize what you must do.

You have no choice. Join him in the circle *ON PAGE 129*

104

The Bishop's staff glows bright red. You run diagonally away from him, zig-zagging to avoid being hit. If you can time it just right...

PEW!

The beam smashes into your side, throwing you across the room. You slide ten feet on the floor before stopping against the glass dome framework.

"Ugh..." you moan.

Craig is on the other side of the dome yelling to you, but you're too woozy to pay attention to him. On the other side of the glass wall is a giant squid. You focus on it as it drifts through the murky water. That's more entertaining than anything in the dome, anyways. You're an Oceanographer. Sea life is what you prefer to focus on. That's what you *thought* you were coming here for.

Eventually Craig stops shouting. You think he got away. But as the Bishop's shadow falls over you, it's as clear as glass that you are at...

THE END

Before you have a chance to answer, Craig blurts out, "The answer is Ecuador!"

"What?"

"It's Ecuador!" His face lights up with confidence. "Equator is even in the name!"

You hesitate. "Wait a second, Craig. The question was which country does the equator *not* pass through!"

His smile wavers. "Oh. Oh *no.*"

The computer voice returns, with a high-pitched buzzing sound behind it, like a fan spinning out of control:

> *"Incorrect answer. INCORRECT! Critical failure of test. Insufficient processing power to calculate reason for–memory overload. System dump. Coolant failure."*

The high-pitched sound continues to rise. The air vibrates all around you. You throw your hands over your ears to block it out, but it's everywhere!

Just when you think there's going to be an explosion, the ringing ceases.

In fact, *everything* ceases. All the lights in the dome suddenly go out, plunging you in darkness. The sea life beyond the dome is quiet and peaceful.

"What happened?"

"I think we broke the system," Craig says.

You go to the door to Dome Three. It obviously doesn't open. "Okay. So we just wait for someone from the surface to come fix it, right?"

Craig shakes his head. "We can't even figure out how to reproduce most of this, let alone fix it!"

You want to ask what he means, but you're beginning to panic. You feel a tightness in your chest, and the huge open space begins to frighten you. Agoraphobia, the fear of wide open spaces, you remember. You go to the nearest wall and look out at the sea life scurrying across the sandy bottom. Hopefully Craig doesn't know what he's talking about. Someone *has* to come fix the research habitat, right? In any case, for now this is...

THE END

106

You follow the slime into the next room. Unfortunately, it's a dead end: all the walls are doorless except the one you came through. The trail of slime ends in the center of the room, where a black statue of a snail sits. It's barely the size of your fist.

"Whelp, this was a wrong way," Craig says. "Let's go ahead and–"

"Look," you say, pointing. There's something shiny in the slime trail by the statue, reflecting the light from the dome overhead. You take a step forward, until Craig grabs your arm.

"Are you sure you want to do that?" he says.

"I've swam with hammerheads in the Caribbean, and dove inside steel cages to come face-to-face with great whites. I'm not afraid of a statue of a snail, or its mucous slime." Before Craig can stop you, you stride forward and stick your hand in the muck.

It's every bit as disgusting as you expected, like old gelatin. Your hand wraps around something solid, and you pull it loose.

The object has a short handle, with an end shaped like a three-dimensional pentagon. Groove are set into each side's face in random configurations. It almost looks like a futuristic...

"Key!" Craig says. "That's a key! I remember seeing photos of that, from one of the previous attempts."

"Attempts?"

Craig blinks, then scratches his head. "*Tests.* I meant tests."

You wipe the key on Craig's sleeve, spreading slime from his elbow to his wrist. Ignoring his cries of protest, you grin and say, "Hopefully this comes in handy later."

You've found the pentagon shaped key! You might need it later.

Return to the urchin room *ON PAGE 138*

After finishing off the goblin with your sword, the hologram blade feels powerful in your hand–even if it *isn't* real. With a wordless cry you charge forward, sword raised high.

You get halfway to his horse before a thick bolt of energy shoots from the end of the staff, striking you directly in the chest. Somehow, inexplicably, you feel it! It stops your charge dead in its tracks and throws you onto your back.

"What the..." you mutter, staring at the dome ceiling far above.

Craig rushes over to see if you're okay. You accept his help getting to your feet. "I think so. That's some game!"

"Yeah, we'd make a fortune if we could figure out how to reproduce it, and sell it."

Before you can ask what he means, there's a trembling in the ground. The three screens flicker, and then turn an ominous shade of scarlet. Steel clamps rise out of the ground and snag your ankles, holding you in place. A voice calls out, calm and robotic. You can't tell what the source is, but it seems to come from inside your own mind.

"Subjects: inadequate. Full system shutdown."

"I've never seen *this* before," Craig says. "Everyone else got farther!"

"What do you mean, farther?"

The screens cut off, removing the red glow. Everything returns to normal.

Except for, you know, the restraints clamped to your ankles.

You can't move, which means you can't proceed. Will you get rescued? The other scientists have to come down eventually, right? But even if they do, you're stuck for now, which means you're at...

THE END

108

"The answer is the causality neutrino."

"How do you know that?" Craig asks.

"I read it somewhere."

Sure enough, the tablet begins to change. The letters on its surface swirl and warp until it's nothing but smooth stone. The ground groans, and with the grinding sound of rock-on-rock the tablet descends into the mountain. When it's gone, you have a clear view of the third mountain. Another tablet stands there, beckoning you with blue light. Its peak is below yours, and closer than you previously thought.

"I think we need to jump."

"Yeah." Craig gulps audibly. "I think so."

It's a long way, but you're pretty sure you can make it. As long as some bad luck doesn't stop you...

FLIP TWO COINS!

If they both land heads, *GO TO PAGE 14*
Otherwise, *FLIP TO PAGE 55*

Abruptly, the blue lines begin to expand into the damaged area, filling in the gaps. It's like a neon spiderweb, growing from the efforts of hundreds of giant spiders. The blue lines form equilateral triangles, building them out and around the far end of the dome. Soon the two halves meet, connecting together with flashes of light.

The color inside the dome begins to change, beginning at the very top. It takes you a long while to realize what's happening.

"The water is draining from the dome!" Craig says, taking the words out of your mouth.

You watch as the water level descends. It's not long before the dome is fully drained and looking like normal. The walls and ceiling darken, returning them to their previous state, blocking your view.

The door opens horizontally, allowing you inside.

You take one cautious step forward. There are walls all around you, with only a few feet of space on either side. This is in stark contrast to the huge open areas of the previous domes.

Glancing at the ceiling, you realize you can see the reflection of the room off the glass. You squint, and your mouth hangs open.

"Craig, this dome is a maze!"

Hopefully there's no minotaur named Kavalgyth. *GO TO PAGE 128*

MYSTERY IN THE MURKY DEEP

110

You couldn't tell from the submarine, but now that your perspective is different you realize the domes are *huge*. It's like being inside a basketball stadium. The shell is almost entirely glass, hundreds of large triangles, with black girders spiderwebbing in between them for framework. The glass seems to give off light, so much that you realize you're squinting while your eyes adjust. Above and to your right you see a school of fish swimming by, a reminder that you're thousands of feet underwater.

"Wow," Craig says, drawing the word out into three syllables. "I've seen pictures, but they do not do it justice. Not at all."

You lower your gaze to the center of the room. It's mostly empty space, except for two raised platforms, shaped like small volcanoes with flat surfaces on the top. Steps are built into the side. Beyond them, on the opposite wall, is a door marked: DOME TWO. Its light is green!

Eager to get this over with, you head straight for the door. Expecting it to open automatically, you walk forward confidently–and bump right into its surface.

"Ow!"

Craig scratches the back of his head. "Sorry. Should have warned you. The doors only open if we complete the tests first.

You approach the first platform and climb the steps. They're made of the same carbon polymer Craig was talking about, and you feel your shoes sink in a fraction of an inch. It's strangely unsettling.

You reach the top. Before you are three glass screens, like the largest televisions you've ever seen. They form three sides of a square, with the open side facing you.

"Oh no," Craig moans. "This is all wrong."

"What do you mean?"

"The screens are normally on. Right now it looks like they're powered off. If the other scientists damaged it..."

You peer over the edge and see a thick cable attached to the base of the platform. You follow it with your eyes to where it meets up with the other platform's cable, and then disappears into the wall.

"Look, I think it's disconnected!" you say.

Craig follows you down the steps and over to where the cable meets the wall. Sure enough, it's unplugged.

"Which port does it connect to?"

Craig shrugs. "Like I said, I'm just a boring administrator. Action movies taught me to always cut the red wire instead of the blue one, but they never said anything about power plugs..."

"This isn't an action movie," you mutter, examining the cable.

Which port should you plug it into?

To choose the top port, *GO TO PAGE 76*
If you think it's the middle port, *TURN TO PAGE 86*
If the bottom port looks correct, *FLIP TO PAGE 96*

112

"Proton!" you call out. It feels like the right answer.

The writing on the tablet suddenly melts away, leaving a smooth surface. You touch the stone. How did that happen?

There's a rumbling sound, which you feel in your shoes. It's coming from inside the mountain!

You're about to yell "Run!" when the ground opens up beneath you. You plummet into darkness.

It feels like you fall for an eternity, but it's probably only a few seconds. You land on something spongy and soft, like a memory foam pillow. You get the distinct impression it's the same black material everything else in the habitat is made of.

You get to your feet in the darkness. The only light is from the opening high above.

"I guess proton was wrong," Craig says.

The two of you feel around in the darkness, but there's no way out that you can find. The mountain is hollow, and you're trapped inside! You feel like a fly captured underneath a drinking glass. But who did the trapping, and what will they do when they come find you? You're beginning to suspect it's not what you originally thought.

But hey, you'll have a lot of time to think about it while you wait, because you've reached...

THE END

"Callisto," you say.

The entire mountain trembles. You get the impression that it's an *angry* trembling, too.

"No! Callisto is an inert moon, whose interior is comprised of compact ice and rock! The Callistii are boring, uninformed–test subjects failed. Complete failure."

The voice cuts off. For a moment you're too shocked to speak. Despite the tone, the voice sounded downright emotional!

"Uh oh," Craig says. Above you, a dark shape is approaching the exterior of the dome. You squint at the vaguely familiar shape.

"Oh my gosh," you say just before it crashes through the glass. "That's a *whale!*"

The glass and black framework of the dome explodes inward, with the roar of water behind it. The dome quickly begins to flood.

But your eyes are glued to the disappearing whale as it swims away. "We're too deep for a whale. They're mammals. It would need to come up for air."

"Forget about the whale, what are *we* going to do?"

Craig's right. The water level is halfway up the jagged mountain, and rising fast. It will reach you in a few seconds.

You're trapped. You have no hope to escape. But you can't stop thinking about that whale. Was it real, or some sort of hologram like many of the other things down here? Maybe you'll find out another time, but not *this* time, since this is...

THE END

114

You point to a spot on the board. "Place it here."

"Are you sure?"

"I think so."

Hesitantly, Craig moves his hand toward the board. The hologram shimmers in his palm. As he nears the square you chose, the triangle *shoots* out of his hand and attaches to the board like a magnet.

PEW!

The blue laser shoots toward the board. It bounces off the first mirror, then another. Then it strikes the mirror you placed...

...and careens off the board and toward the ceiling! You watch in horror as it strikes the dome high above, shattering it into a thousand tiny pieces.

WHOOSH!

Water immediately gushes into the dome like a waterfall. Your ears pop as the pressure in the room changes rapidly. Craig cries out.

"That was the wrong one!"

Within seconds, the dome is flooded five feet. It's rising quickly, and you're trapped on the platform!

"I knew I should have stayed in my office. Papers and files are boring, but at least they're *safe.*"

You watch the water grow closer. You're paralyzed by indecision. For a moment you think about swimming to the door, but it's already underwater.

You're out of options. Worse, you got Craig into this! As the water soaks your shoes you accept that this is...

THE END

Blue is better than red. Right? Confidently, you yank the blue wire until the exposed part comes free of the computer screen.

It's the wrong thing to do, and you immediately know it. The lights in the long tunnel change to a sinister red, and the voice blares from everywhere at once:

"Security intrusion detected. Tamper protection initiated."

"What does tamper–" you begin to ask Craig, cutting off as you see walls dropping down from the ceiling, dividing the hallway into individual segments. One *whooshes* through the air between you two, slamming into the ground with a hollow bang.

The lights stop flashing, leaving you in darkness.

You bang on the wall, calling Craig's name, but there's no response. The black, spongy material seems to absorb all vibration and sound. Still, you pound away for what feels like hours, waiting for rescue. Maybe it will come. Someone *has* to come check on you, right? But it's a long wait until then, and in the mean time you need to accept that you've made a mistake resulting in an abrupt version of...

THE END

116

The goblin has almost reached you. It lifts the axe high above his head, preparing a vicious overhand swing.

You bring up your shield, protecting your face. The goblin is visible through the hologram shield. A wicked snarl spreads across its face.

The axe comes down smack in the middle of your shield.

Despite being a hologram, the force somehow sends you stumbling backward, nearly losing your balance. The goblin swings again and again, axe head hammering dents in the shield, pushing you back to the edge of the platform. You stop yourself before falling over the edge.

With a final swing the goblin's axe breaks the shield in two, the halves sliding off your arm to clatter to the floor. You wince, preparing for it to finish you off.

But the goblin ends his volley of strikes. He steps back and jumps up in down in silent victory.

Abruptly, the hologram disappears: the goblin, your sword and armor, the broken shield. Everything is gone in the blink of an eye as the screens turn off. Then there's a voice, which seems to come from everywhere and nowhere all at once, like it's speaking in your imagination:

"Subject: failure. Proceed to next dome."

The screens go blank. Across the room, the door to Dome Two suddenly opens.

You turn to Craig. "I never was good at videogames."

"I can see that."

"But hey," you say, "it opened the door to the next dome. That's good, right?"

"I guess so," Craig says, though he doesn't sound convinced.

Oh well. Proceed to Dome Two by *TURNING TO PAGE 120*

You raise your sword just as the knight swings, parrying his blow. The sound of steel on steel rings through the hollow dome.

Your opponent is quick. He turns your deflection into a sideways swing, which glances off your shield. Then he thrusts: you swing your own sword down, knocking it aside.

Hey, I'm pretty good at this! you think.

The knight takes a moment to breathe, surprised by your skill. Then he's charging forward again, raising his blade and cutting diagonally across his body. You take a step back and swing sideways, pushing the sword just out of range of your body. Then, while the knight is off-balance, you strike a final blow into his back.

The blade goes right through him, because it's a hologram. For a moment you had forgotten. It was so real!

The knight stops fighting the moment the blade touches him. He stands up straight and raises the visor of his helm. He gives you a respectful nod, and before you can return the gesture he's suddenly gone. *All* of it is gone: the knight, the scenery on the three screens, even your own holographic sword, shield, and armor.

A happy sound chimes in the air. A robotic voice calls out, so close that it feels like they're in your own mind:

"Station: complete. Proceed to next test."

"Nice job!" Craig says, wiping sweat from his forehead. "That was exciting. Way more exciting than sitting in my office."

"I must have been Joan of Arc in another life," you say. You can't believe how well you did!

Across the room, the second platform abruptly lights up.

"I don't know what these tests are for," you say, "but I guess we'd better move on to the next one."

Are you ready for the next test? *HEAD TO PAGE 124*

118

This one is a little bit trickier, but you've got the hang of it. After careful examination of the puzzle, and double-checking that you're right, you place the mirror onto the square.

PEW!

Blue lights glows all around you as the laser bounces through the grid, striking the mirrors and deflecting back and forth. And, after several 90 degree turns, it hits the circle on the right.

Craig pats you on the back. "Yeah!"

But something else is happening. At first you think it's the grid rearranging itself for a third time. You're wrong. This time it's the *circle* that's changing, rotating until the edge faces you. It spins, faster and faster, until it's moving like a coin spinning on a table. You hold your breath, waiting to see what it will do.

The blue light shoots toward your face, blinding you momentarily. You cry out, but something keeps your feet firmly in place. Maybe it's fear.

The hiss of the laser stops. You blink, and the grid and lasers all disappear.

"What was tha–" Craig cuts off. He points at your forehead. "It marked your forehead!"

You close your mouth. You were about to say the same thing to Craig! There's a strange symbol printed on his skin:

You describe it to Craig. "What does it mean?"

"I don't know," he says, "but at least it doesn't hurt. Come on, let's go to Dome Two before it happens again!"

You realize the door out of the dome is open, waiting for you.

Hopefully it's not permanent! *ENTER ON PAGE 120*

There's a long moment of silence after you give your answer. You feel unseen eyes watching you.

"Incorrect. Subjects disqualified. Proceed to Dome Three."

The three-sided stone suddenly moves, disappearing down into the ground. When it's done nothing remains but a flat surface.

"If we're disqualified, why do we get to proceed? Does Dome Three lead back to the surface somehow?"

"I'm just an administrator..." Craig begins. You roll your eyes and begin climbing down the mountain.

Sure enough, the door marked DOME THREE is wide open. The tunnel beckons you forward.

Explore Dome Three *ON PAGE 130*

120

The tunnel is much the same as the first one, made of that same spongy black material as everything else. It feels like your footsteps should echo, but you can't hear much, almost as if the black material is absorbing all the sound. There are no windows here, and while walking to the other end you almost forget you're several thousand feet underwater.

You come to the door, which slides open into the wall at your approach. You step into the room.

Dome Two is both the same, and completely different, as Dome One. Although roughly the same size and shape, the architecture of the dome isn't made up of triangular windows connected with framework. This dome *has* no framework. It looks like one enormous bubble of glass, without edge or seam.

"How is that possible?" you say.

"What's that, Jessica?"

"Without reinforcement, the water pressure this deep should crush the dome like an empty soda can. And even ignoring that, why is it different than the first dome? Why not construct them the same way? Were they built at different times?" You begin to think about the flooded Dome Three. Maybe the difference in construction is what caused that one to fail?

"Those are very good questions," Craig says slowly. He bobs his head. "*Very* good questions."

"You mean you don't know the answer?"

"Nope! I don't. I don't think anyone has figured that out yet."

Instead of raised platforms, this dome has the inverse: three pits sunk into the ground, like inside-out cones. One of them is illuminated in bright spotlights. The other two are dark.

Since it's obvious you're not going to get any answers out of Craig, you step toward the first pit. Steps are built into the sloped wall.

Enter the first pit and *DESCEND TO PAGE 35*

The knight looks like he's about to swing, so you raise your shield in anticipation of the strike. But just as you do, he raises his own shield and bulls into you!

The blow throws you backward, and you slide three feet along the ground. Before you can get up the knight stands over you, pointing his sword at your head. He gives a final nod of sportsmanship.

Before he can finish you off, though, he suddenly disappears. One moment he was there, and then the next all you see is the ceiling of the dome.

Craig is there in a hurry, pulling you to your feet. "You were so close!"

The three screens have already turned off, returning the platform to boring normalcy. A voice cuts the air, seemingly coming from everywhere all at once, like it's speaking in your imagination:

"Subject: failure. Proceed to next dome."

Across the room, the door to Dome Two suddenly opens. You blink in surprise.

"Proceed? But I lost. What kind of a test is that?"

"Well..." Craig begins. "It's complicated."

"How about you try to explain it to me?" you ask.

"Let's just move on," he says. "We need to get to Dome Three and figure out what happened." He descends the steps off the platform.

You follow, wondering what he's not telling you. You also glance at the second platform, wondering what kind of test it would have given.

Nice try. Check out Dome Two *ON PAGE 120*

122

You pick up the Queen with two fingers and move her vertically, taking the black player's pawn. But the King remains out of danger.

"Aww, I thought–" you begin, until the chess piece sends a zap of electricity up your arm.

"OW!"

You drop the piece, but it flickers. That's when you realize it's just a hologram. The board flickers as well and then resets itself to the original configuration.

You glare at Craig.

"Hey, err, look!" he says awkwardly. "We get another chance! Wish I had joined the chess club in school..."

To move the Queen diagonally, *GO TO PAGE 126*
To move the Queen horizontally, *GO TO PAGE 52*

"It's Galileo. He discovered Jupiter's four largest moons. That's why they're called the Galilean moons!"

Sure enough, the stone begins to rotate again, bringing the third and final face around. It causes the entire mountaintop to tremble. You try to regain your balance, even though a wave of vertigo washes over you. It's strange being on top of a rocky peak, while inside of a bubble of air at the bottom of the ocean!

"They're called the Galilean moons," you continue when the trembling stops. "Jupiter has dozens of moons, but those are the largest–"

Craig cuts you off. "Looks like the next question is about them." You read the carved words on the slab:

OF JUPITER'S LARGEST MOONS, WHICH ONE IS THE MOST VOLCANIC IN THE SOLAR SYSTEM?

"Why are the tests so obsessed with Jupiter?" you mutter.

"Or maybe it heard you talking about the moons, and decided to quiz you," Craig suggests.

You blink. "What do you mean? I thought these were pre-programmed questions."

He gives you a blank look and then turns his attention to the slab.

You feel awfully unsettled by the conversation. Plus, the questions are *carved* into the rock. You decide that Craig must be pulling your leg.

"Okay," you say, "the most volcanic of the moons..."

To guess Io, *FLIP TO PAGE 84*
To say Europa, *SLIDE TO PAGE 119*
To answer Ganymede, *JUMP TO PAGE 135*
To respond Callisto, *GO TO PAGE 113*

124

You jump up the steps to the second platform. It's just like the first, except this one only has *one* computer screen. It's the size of a whiteboard from one of your classrooms, except it's made of clear glass.

It's also completely blank.

"So... what do we do?" you say.

Craig shrugs. "I don't know why you keep asking me. I told you..."

You take a step toward the screen, and that does the trick. It flickers like a television turning on, and then a dozen lasers shoot horizontally across the screen. Vertical lines appear next, creating a checkerboard pattern. In some of the squares are other shapes, like triangles. On the left is a blue cylinder pointed toward the board. On the right is a blue circle, like a sideways basketball hoop without the net.

"This isn't like any game I've ever seen," you say. "What *is* it?"

PEW!

As if on command, the cylinder on the left flashes. It shoots a blue laser toward the board, where it bounces off one of the triangles, changing directions at a right-angle. It bounces off another triangle before fizzling off the board.

Craig snaps his fingers. "I think I understand!" He points to the blue circle on the right. "The laser needs to go *here*. We have to make it bounce off the triangle mirrors around the board so that it does."

"How do we do that?"

Suddenly, a hologram triangle appears in Craig's hand. He flinches and shakes his hand, but it won't go away.

"I guess we have to place this one triangle mirror on the board, to deflect the laser into the circle."

You stare at the board. "Just *one?* I mean, I could figure it out if we had two or three, but one..."

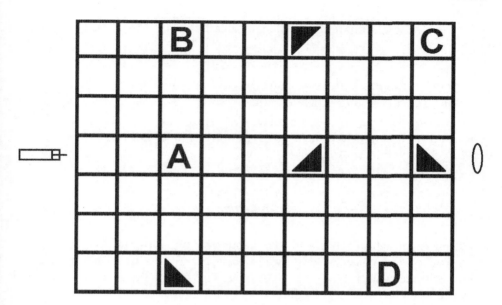

Craig swallows. "Well. Where do we place it? I don't like the look of these lasers..."

Where should you place the triangle mirror to deflect the laser to the end?

To place it in square **A,** *GO TO PAGE 114*
To place it in square **B,** *GO TO PAGE 131*
To place it in square **C,** *GO TO PAGE 160*
To place it in square **D,** *GO TO PAGE 166*
If you're unsure, *KICK THE SCREEN ON PAGE 149*

126

You grab the Queen and give Craig a sarcastic grin. "*This* time, I'm going to move her–"

ZAP!

You drop the piece and recoil your hand. It shocked you!

"But I didn't even move the piece yet!"

To your surprise, a voice responds. It's electronic and soothing, and you can't quite tell if it's a man or a woman. It speaks softly, but you hear it clearly, as if it's speaking directly into your ear:

> *"We knew your move. It was incorrect. Test subjects to be collected for later examination."*

"Later examination?" You put your hands on your hips and look around for the source of the voice. "Okay, listen. This isn't funny anymore. If someone doesn't tell me what's going on right now I'm getting back on the sub and returning to the surface."

"Uhh... I don't think we have that option."

You turn to see what he's talking about. The chess board is shrinking, and one piece growing. It's the enemy King, dressed in obsidian robes and holding a scepter. The crown on his head is half-buried in his thick brown hair. Within seconds he's the same size as you.

"What the..."

He steps forward and wraps you and Craig in his arms, pulling you close. You thought it was just a hologram, but he feels awfully real. In fact, it feels like he's made of the same spongy black material from the habitat.

Craig starts pounding on the King's chest, so you do the same. His grip is *strong*. You can barely breathe, let alone escape!

"Let go of us!" you cry.

The King carries you away from the green ring and toward another door that opens in the floor, revealing stairs going down. You cry louder but it's no use: whatever it is, it's not listening. You don't know where he's taking you, or what kind of examination it will be, but you do know that help isn't coming. And without help, you cannot advance, which means you are at...

THE END

"I hate math, so physics wins by default." You stride over to the second mountain and grab onto the first hand-hold. It sure *feels* like a real mountain. How did they get it to the bottom of the ocean?

You begin climbing, one hand over the other. There always seems to be a place to grab onto waiting wherever your hand goes. After a minute or so you reach the top, a flat surface twenty feet across.

On it is a giant stone tablet, as big as a door.

Craig climbs up next to you, brushing off his shirt. "Woah," he says.

"Okay, now I'm impressed," you say. "I have no idea how any of this was constructed so far under the sea. That slab has to weigh a ton!"

You step up to it and see that letters are carved onto its surface, faintly glowing blue. For a split second they seem to be in every language at once, but then you blink and they're in English.

WHAT IS THE NAME OF THE SUBATOMIC PARTICLE RESPONSIBLE FOR AN ATOM'S POSITION IN TIME?

You look around at the mountain and the slab of rock. "This is an awful lot of work just for a trivia question."

Craig nods to himself. "Now you're getting it." Before you can ask more, he says, "Do you know the answer? I don't."

Well? Do you?

If the particle is a **proton,** *GO TO PAGE 112*
If the particle is a **causality neutrino,** *GO TO PAGE 108*
If the particle is an **electron,** *TURN TO PAGE 91*

Fed-up with the research habitat? Knock the tablet over *TO PAGE 59*

128

You're at the maze entrance. It's shaped like a square, with doors on each wall leading away in four directions. The door out of the maze, however, is closed shut.

The walls are made of the same black, spongy material as everything else. The glow of the dome ceiling casts everything in a frightful light.

Above each door is a carving, almost unnoticeable at first. You realize they're carvings of animals. They remind you of the stone gargoyles on European cathedrals.

To the east is a door with a peacock.

To the south is a door with a dolphin.

To the west is a door with an sea urchin.

"This reminds me of my old days playing text-based videogames," Craig says nervously. "Except in those games we always had swords and shields..."

Alright. Which way do you want to go?

For the peacock room, *GO TO PAGE 165*
If you want to follow the dolphin, *TURN TO PAGE 32*
To choose the urchin room, *FLIP TO PAGE 138*

With a mixture of fear and concern, you step into the red circle with Craig. As you've experienced all day, a computerized voice rings out in your mind, soothing and calm.

"Subjects: present. Beginning test result data analysis."

You close your eyes as the alien computer scans you and Craig. It feels like everything that has happened in the habitat, all the tests and scans and quizzes, have led to this exact moment.

You try not to tremble. You fail.

Okay, think back! How many symbols have been burned into your forehead?

If you have **ZERO** symbols, *GO TO PAGE 194*
If you have **ONE** symbol, *GO TO PAGE 170*
If you have **TWO** symbols, *GO TO PAGE 136*
If you have **THREE** symbols, *GO TO PAGE 142*

130

The tunnel into Dome Three is just like all the others, but you have a tingling sense of foreboding. Your steps echo ominously as you approach the end.

You stop in front of the door. Of course, it doesn't open. Because the dome is flooded. For a moment you feel silly.

"So, uhh, now what?" you ask. There's a panel that looks like a computer screen on the wall, but it's presently turned off.

Craig obviously has no idea what to do. He stares at the door, then looks around as if there's another way.

"Seriously? You brought me down here and you have no idea what to do?"

"Well... I mean, I *thought* I knew. But I think I'm wrong."

You stare back the way you came. "Maybe we need to backtrack. Try one of the domes we haven't been inside yet."

As you twist around, the computer screen on the wall flickers. A vertical blue laser shoots out at you, making you wince.

"Scanning subjects."

The laser moves from the right side of your face to your left. It does the same for Craig.

Quick, think back! Do you have any markings on your forehead?

If so, *PASS THROUGH TO PAGE 148*
If not, *STICK AROUND ON PAGE 133*

Craig's looking at you for direction. It's clear he won't be of any help. You examine the board, imagining where the laser will travel. You point to one spot.

"There."

Hesitantly, Craig reaches forward with the hologram triangle. As his hand nears the square you chose, the mirror is *sucked* onto the board like a magnet. Craig lets out a small yelp. There's a second of pause, and then the blue laser fires again.

PEW!

The laser shoots across the board, bouncing around so fast you can barely keep up. You follow the beam with your eyes as best as you can...

...to where it strikes the wall of the board, fizzling out.

"Aww man," you say.

Craig slumps his head. You can tell he's disappointed.

The screen makes an unhappy noise, and the lights of the screen and platform go out. A voice calls out from some unseen speaker, which must be in the floor because it sounds like it's coming from all around you at once:

"Subject: failure. Proceed to next dome."

The door across the room opens.

"Huh. I guess we still get to move on?" you say. "So we were still successful!"

"I guess," Craig said, sounding anything but certain.

Weird. *PROCEED TO PAGE 120*

132

You go through the instructions over and over. Each time you think it's a different wire.

"We're running out of time," Craig warns. The clock is at 20 seconds.

Panicked, you quickly cut wire three.

KABOOM!

There's a flash of light and you're thrown across the dome, landing hard on your back. It knocks the wind out of you. It takes several moments before you're able to gasp your first breath. Then everything goes black.

You wake up to blue sky.

"What the..."

You're back on the surface vessel. Everyone is standing around you: Craig, and all the other scientists that were on the other sub. They look concerned, until Craig lets out a long breath.

"Thank goodness you're okay, Jessica! When you cut the wrong wire..."

The geologist crosses his arms. "Cut the wrong wire? What kind of tests are down there?"

"It's hard to explain," you mutter.

Geologist rolls his eyes. "I'm sure it's not that difficult. Come on." He and the other scientists climb aboard the sub.

After the medical officer makes sure you're okay–except for a headache–they call for a helicopter. Craig stays with you as you fly back to California. He tells you how exciting the research habitat was, and that he wished you two had progressed further.

You lean your head back on the cushion. It feels good to just relax and close your eyes. You begin to think about the class midterm you have to plan. You have so much work to catch up on! The beating of the rotors rocks you to sleep as you return home.

THE END

The laser moves across your face in a slow scan. It pauses for a minute, then scans across again as if disappointed in the first result.

"Subjects: failed. Access denied."

"Failed? What did we fail?" you say.

Craig looks disappointed. "I thought for sure with your help we could pass. After all the others that couldn't solve this place..."

You ignore his cryptic comment. Gripping the computer screen, you yank until it rips free from the wall.

"Hey! Don't do that!"

A bundle of wires leads from the back of the screen into the wall. "I dabbled in IT when I was an undergrad," you say. "I should be able to find a way to..."

You trail off as you get a good look inside the wall. The circuitry is unlike anything you've ever seen! Though it shouldn't surprise you, considering the technology you've already seen down here.

Following the wires, you nod to yourself. "There's eight wires here. These six–" you hold up a bundle, "–are data only. Which leaves the other two for display and security. All we have to do is cut the security wire."

"So which one's the security wire?" Craig asks. You can tell he's nervous about the whole thing.

You examine the wires. One is red, the other blue. Which should you remove?

To disconnect the RED wire, *FLIP TO PAGE 139*
If you think the BLUE wire is the one, *GO TO PAGE 115*

134

You look down at your tower shield. Its surface is as reflective as a mirror. An idea comes to you.

The wizard smiles smugly as a bolt of energy shoots from the end of his staff. You raise your shield to protect your face.

PING!

The bolt of energy bounces off the shield harmlessly. You barely even feel it! And even better, it reflects back at the wizard! He drops his staff with a curse. The long piece of wood is now charred black with tendrils of smoke rising into the air.

The wizard looks furious. For a moment you think the battle isn't over, but then he fades away, horse and all.

"Woah," Craig says.

Before you can enjoy your victory, you hear the sound of metal on metal, like a bag of bolts bouncing around. You turn to the right screen and see an armored knight staring at you! He's dressed identical to you, with plate mail and a sword and shield. He rests the sword on his shoulder casually.

You turn to face him. He waits until you're ready, then gives a polite nod, lowers his sword, and advances with careful steps.

This feels like the final fight. How will you defeat the knight?

To dodge the knight's swing, *JUMP ASIDE TO PAGE 44*
To raise your sword, *SWING TO PAGE 117*
To block with your shield, *HIDE BEHIND PAGE 121*

You feel a subtle, almost imperceptible wind. It's like a disappointed exhale from a giant. Then the voice you heard earlier speaks:

"Incorrect. Subjects: failed. Proceed to next dome for further testing."

The voice sounds impatient.

Without warning, the gargantuan stone slab begins sinking into the ground, grinding loudly. When it's fully beneath the rock its top becomes a smooth, seamless surface with the rest of the peak.

Across the room, you can see that the door marked DOME THREE now stands open.

"At least we can keep going," Craig says.

"*Keep* going? What would have happened otherwise?" His comment doesn't make any sense to you.

Craig doesn't answer. Instead, he starts climbing down the mountain to the dome floor. Carefully, you follow.

Enter Dome Three *ON PAGE 130*

136

The laser moves across your forehead, from your left ear to your right, then back again. The computer beeps.

"Data analysis complete..."

Okay, hopefully you were taking notes! What was the first symbol you received?

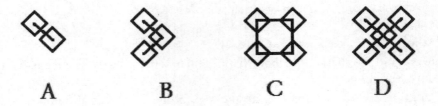

A   **B**   **C**   **D**

If it was symbol **A**, *GO TO PAGE 184*
If it was symbol **B**, *TURN TO PAGE 174*
If it was symbol **C**, *FLIP TO PAGE 178*
If it was symbol **D**, *HEAD TO PAGE 188*

You're feeling pretty confident after your first success. You quickly examine the board, then extend your hand to one of the squares.

Craig says, "Wait, I think–"

It's too late: the mirror flies from your hand to attach to the square. The laser hums, glows, and fires.

PEW!

It's immediately clear you made the wrong choice. The laser bounces off two mirrors and then shoots toward the floor, striking the power cable leading to the screen.

KA-BOOM!

You're thrown backwards, flying over the edge of the platform and onto the ground. It knocks the wind out of you, and for several agonizing seconds you struggle just to breathe.

Then you suck in a little bit of air, trickling into your lungs. Slowly, one breath at a time, you begin to feel normal.

But as you stand up, you realize that your head still feels dizzy. Everything is moving, even the floor! You reach out to balance yourself–and fall right back on your face.

You're drifting off to sleep now, into pleasant unconsciousness. Don't worry; you'll wake eventually. Craig will probably find help, and then the two of you will escape. But you *won't* be progressing further into the habitat, which means you are now at...

THE END

138

The urchin room looks the same as the last one, except for the small spiny statue in the middle of the room. It's incredibly life-like, so much so that you are afraid to touch it.

You take a deep breath and look around. There are only two options, unless you suddenly find a grappling hook and rope.

To the east is a blank doorway. It leads to the maze entrance room, you remember.

To the west is a door with a snail. The floor has a trail of menacing-looking slime leading inside.

"So, uhh," Craig says. "Which way do we go?" He says it in a way that makes it obvious he doesn't want to decide.

To enter the snail room, *SLIDE TO PAGE 106*
If you want to return to the maze entrance, *GO TO PAGE 128*

Your hands are shaking as you grip the red wire between your finger and thumb. What will happen if you're wrong?

Only one way to find out.

The red wire comes away smoothly. The screen immediately flickers, and you hold it up to look. Strange symbols scroll across, like the ones marked on your foreheads. The symbols twist and deform, like sand being swirled by a finger. Then they change into recognizable letters: you see Russian characters, then Latin ones, in languages like Portuguese and French. Finally the words become English, and as if the computer can sense that that's the right language, it stops.

The screen shows three options:

- ENABLE AUTOMATIC REPAIR -
- DIAGNOSTICS INFORMATION -
- EXIT SHIP -

"Well that's a relief." Craig scratches his head and readjusts his glasses. "Huh. Exit ship?"

"It must be the same program that the submarines use," you say. "Right? Nothing else makes sense."

"Maybe," Craig says. "I'm not sure what we should do..."

It looks like it's up to you to decide.

To Enable Automatic Repair, *GO TO PAGE 159*
If you want to see Diagnostics Information, *FLIP TO PAGE 168*
Or, if you want to try the Exit Ship option, *MOVE TO PAGE 92*

140

After being in the cavernous dome, the tight tunnel seems claustrophobic by comparison. It feels like your head is going to brush the ceiling. Who designed these tunnels to be so short? When the door at the end opens to Dome Four, it's a welcome sight.

It's the same general size as Dome Five, but that's where the similarities end. Instead of glass triangles, this dome is made of glass *pentagons*, with black girders in between. Why on earth would they make two domes in different ways?

But what really catches your attention are the contents of the dome. Two tall mountains stand before you, brown and steep, like rocky traffic cones. A third is visible behind the first two.

"Woah..." Craig says. "I haven't seen this dome."

"I thought you've seen pictures?"

"Well, yes. But Dome Four is usually sports equipment. Throwing balls and javelins and stuff."

You turn to face him. "Wait, are you telling me this dome has completely changed? These mountains just *appeared* out of thin air?"

He gets an uncomfortable look on his face. "Well, it's not that simple. The domes are unpredictable. The research habitat behaves erratically."

"You're acting like the habitat has a mind of its own."

He gives a noncommittal shrug, and says no more.

You sigh and turn back to the mountains. Both have faint holograms on their peaks. The mountain on the left has numerals to symbolize math, and the one on the right has an atom, symbolizing physics.

"So math, or physics." you say. "Those are our choices?"

"Looks like it."

Which mountain would you prefer?

To climb the Math mountain, *GO TO PAGE 143*
If Physics is more your style, *CRAWL TO PAGE 127*

The goblin lunges at the end of his charge, bringing his axe down. You swing your sword sideways to parry the blow. The blade strikes the end of the axe head, but it's too heavy to divert. The axe crashes down...

...and passes harmlessly through you. Good thing it's just a game!

The goblin jumps up and down in victory, and then disappears. The peaceful scene on the screens disappears.

"I guess I need to play more Dungeons and Dragons," you say.

Craig gasps. "What's happening?"

He's right–a trembling is growing in the floor, and the screens are now glowing a disappointing shade of red. It's time to get out of here.

Before you can, metal clamps rise out of the floor and wrap around your ankles. You tug against them. They don't budge.

You're stuck!

"Craig, why is this part of the test?" you ask.

"I don't know!" He's pinned to the ground too, looking around wildly. The red glow casts everything in a harsh, sinister shade.

A voice drifts out of the computer screens, calm and robotic. It sounds like it's speaking directly into your mind.

"Subjects: inadequate. Full system shutdown."

The screens turn off, returning the room to normal light. The trembling in the floor ceases.

You stand there, unable to move, for several breaths.

"Uhh... now what?"

"I don't know!" cries Craig. "Oh, I wish I had stayed in my office! This is too much excitement!"

Maybe you'll be rescued. The other scientists have to come back down eventually, right? You don't know what the videogame was testing, but you feel disappointed at failing.

Your pride has taken a beating, and you won't get any more answers out of the laboratory. This is...

THE END

142

The laser moves across your forehead twice before making an unhappy sounding beep.

"Invalid data. Rescanning."

You glance over at Craig, and he gives you a worried look. What does that mean?

Again the laser scans your forehead, from right to left, and then back again. It makes the same angry beep.

"Subjects proficient in a multitude of skills. Insufficient programming logic to account for this scenario. Initiating emergency procedures. Locking down ship. Deactivating crew stasis."

Suddenly the entire room is flashing red. You guess that's the universal sign for *bad*, huh?

"Locking down the ship?" you say. "This whole thing is a *ship?*"

"JESSICA! Look!"

There's movement on the screen showing the room with the diagonal pods. Icy mist puffs into the air as the first pod opens. One by one the others swing open. The mist obscures the view, and you're terrified of what you'll soon see.

A hand reaches out, grey and inhumanly long. It grips the side of the glass, pulling itself out.

You turn away before you can see more. "Craig, the elevator's gone!"

"Oh man. Oh man!" He spins around. "We've gotta get out of here." He freezes, facing one of the far walls. There's an open hallway in that direction. "Let's go!"

"But it might lead us toward those pods..."

"Yeah," Craig says, "but if we stay here we'll be found for sure!"

He's right. *FOLLOW CRAIG TO PAGE 176*

"Math should be easier than physics," you say, "though it's a shame we don't have the mathematician with us." You stride toward the first mountain and begin climbing. It feels strange climbing a rock face at the bottom of the ocean, but then again, that's not the weirdest thing you've done today.

Thirty sweaty seconds later, you're at the flat peak. It's occupied by a single stone tablet, slightly larger than a door. Carved onto the face are thick symbols, glowing faintly blue inside the stone. They appear pixelated, like something you'd see from an old arcade machine:

"Huh," Craig says next to you. "I guess they want to see how much simple math we know."

"Who is 'they'?" you ask. "I thought *you* were 'they'. If you're not running this research habitat..."

"Let's focus," Craig says, taking a nervous glance at the ground far below. "I just want to get on with this."

Do you know the answer to the math problem? If so, *TURN TO THAT PAGE*
If you don't know, that's okay too. Instead, *GO TO PAGE 59*

144

You throw up your hands. "I don't know. Can you just let us through, please? I don't even know why I'm here!"

There's a long, pregnant silence. You look around, waiting for some sort of sign.

And there is one. Above you, where the pit meets the dome floor, a metal door begins sliding horizontally across the air. It's closing off the pit–with you inside! The voice announces:

"Uncooperative test subject. Holding for later examination."

"Run!"

You grab Craig's arm and pull him up the steps, taking them two at a time. You squeeze through the opening and fall onto the floor of the dome.

BANG.

The metal slams into position with a hollow echo. That was a close one. What would have happened if you had been trapped? Examination by *who*?

However, the door to Dome Three stands wide open. For a moment you don't think it's real.

"I guess let's move forward?"

Craig shrugs. "Hopefully we can."

Ignoring his negative tone, you lead the way into the tunnel.

Try to enter Dome Three *ON PAGE 130*

"I'm *not* playing any games until you tell me what's going on here," you say. "If you're in charge of the research habitat, then why do we have to complete these to advance?"

"*Technically,* I never said we were in charge of the research habitat," he says carefully. "You assumed we were. That's an important distinction."

Will he ever give you a straight answer? Frustrated, you grab the chess board with both hands and flip it over. Pieces go flying through the air–where they flicker like static and disappear.

It was a hologram!

Craig flinches as if something bad is about to happen. "That was probably a bad idea."

The ground begins to tremble. Across the room, the door marked DOME FOUR is standing wide open! The tunnel beyond is dark, with a faint blue glow from the lights in the floor.

"It looks like flipping the table made the door open," you say. "Not such a bad idea, huh? Come on. Let's go."

You sprint across the dome floor without looking to see if Craig is following.

Enter Dome Four *ON PAGE 140*

146

"Mercury, Venus, Earth, Mars, *Jupiter*," you count off on your fingers. "Jupiter is the fifth planet orbiting the sun."

Instead of any noise of confirmation, the stone begins to move. It rotates to show you another face, stone grinding loudly as it moves. You wonder how large and powerful the gears must be to move such an object so easily!

There's another question on the next surface:

WHICH HUMAN ASTRONOMER DISCOVERED JUPITER'S FOUR LARGEST MOONS?

"More Jupiter," you mutter.
"I know this," Craig says. "It's... umm..."

Do you know who it is?

If it's Nicolaus Copernicus, *GO TO PAGE 135*
If you think it's Tycho Brahe, *GAZE TO PAGE 119*
If the answer is Galileo Galilei, *ZOOM TO PAGE 123*

"The equator obviously runs through Ecuador," you say. "That's why it's named that!"

"Brazil is to the right of Ecuador a bit," Craig says, frowning. "So I think it's the same."

His comment makes you certain. "Our answer is Australia. The equator does not pass through Australia."

Another chime rings in the air. The ring you're standing in blinks twice, and then the third ring across the room changes from red to green.

"Alright! On to the last test!"

You and Craig hurry over there, almost trembling with excitement. You don't know what happens when you pass them all, but you can't wait to find out. Maybe then you'll get some answers!

As you near, the shape of a pedestal appears in the middle of the ring. On it is a rectangular box, bigger than a briefcase. It looks like a small suitcase, but all metal.

You examine it carefully, waiting for the computer voice to give you instructions. It never comes.

"I guess we open it," you say, stepping forward. The two latches open with a click, and you tilt the top back on its hinges. The sides fall away and clatter to the floor, revealing the object inside.

You gasp in shock.

What is it? *FIND OUT ON PAGE 162*

148

The laser moves across your face from right to left, then back again. "It's scanning the markings on our foreheads!" Craig says. Out of the corner of your eye you see another laser doing the same for him.

In the blink of an eye the lasers disappear. A calming, robotic voice sounds out:

"Subjects: passed. Access granted."

There's a hum of something computerized, and the screen on the wall turns on. Strange symbols scroll across, like the ones marked on your foreheads. The symbols twist and deform, like sand being swirled by a finger. Then they change into recognizable letters: you see Russian characters, then Latin ones, in languages like Portuguese and French. Finally the words become English, and as if the computer can sense that's the right language, it stops.

The screen shows three options:

- ENABLE AUTOMATIC REPAIR -
- DIAGNOSTICS INFORMATION -
- EXIT SHIP -

Craig scratches his head and readjusts his glasses. "Huh. Exit ship?"

"It must be the same program the submarines use," you say. "Right? Nothing else makes sense."

"Maybe," Craig says. "I'm not sure what we should do..."

It looks like it's up to you to decide.

To Enable Automatic Repair, *GO TO PAGE 159*
If you want to see Diagnostics Information, *FLIP TO PAGE 168*
Or, if you want to try the Exit Ship option, *MOVE TO PAGE 92*

"I don't know which one to choose," you say. "It's too complicated!"

"I don't know either. And I'm usually good with puzzles," Craig says.

All of your frustrations bubble up at once. You were taken away from your classroom by police, suddenly and without any warning. You were sent to the middle of the Pacific Ocean, then sent deep underwater to a laboratory whose purpose you don't understand. And now you have to jump through hoops!

Without thinking, you pull back your foot and kick the screen as hard as you can. The glass rocks back and forth on its stand, careens backwards almost in slow motion, and falls off the back of the platform.

The sound of shattering glass drifts back up to you.

Craig stares at you. For a long moment you're both completely silent. Then he doubles over with laughter.

"Ahha! That was..." He can barely talk, he's laughing so hard. "That... totally unexpected. Never would have..."

You can't help but smile. "Sorry. That must have cost a lot of money."

"Probably, but *we* didn't pay for it," he says.

You're about to ask him what he means when across the room, against the wall, the door to Dome Two opens.

"Subject: failure. Proceed to next dome."

The voice is calm and soothing, and you can't tell where it's coming from. But you don't even care.

"Maybe we get to continue to the next dome because we beat the knight test?"

Craig says, "Maybe so," but he doesn't sound convinced.

Afraid that it might close without warning, you both hurry to the door.

Check out Dome Two and *FLIP TO PAGE 120*

150

You approach the door, which is steel and doesn't have any handle or knob. It looks shockingly smooth, without any features at all. You take a step to examine it closer, and without warning it slides open, disappearing into the wall.

"Pretty high-tech research habitat," you say.

"Yeah, it is." Craig is looking all around with wonder, as if surprised at just how true it is.

The tunnel is completely dark, except for pulsing blue lights recessed into the floor every ten feet. The walls and ceiling are unlike anything you've ever seen: they're black like metal, but not shiny. Dull, like coal. You touch the surface and discover that it's soft!

"It's a special carbon polymer. Or at least, as best as we can tell," Craig says. "Very advanced. It will probably be years before we can develop it for industrial and commercial sale..."

"It reminds me of sea sponges," you observe. "Metallic sea sponges."

It's a while before you reach the door into the dome. It opens automatically, and as you pass through you're treated with a view of the dome interior, the ceiling rising above you.

You gasp.

Admire the view *ON PAGE 156*

"But what were you testing in the first place?" You cross your arms the way you would if talking to a stubborn student. "You aren't answering the root question."

We are performing the standard scouting duties, the head alien says. *The way it has been done for millennia.*

The gills on the other two aliens flare in agreement.

"Scouting for what?"

For intelligence. The tone makes it sound like it's obvious. *Throughout the universe, we search for other life that is intelligent. Life is abundant. Life is everywhere. But it is usually minuscule in size and capability, such as the life on your planet Jupiter. A small percentage are multicellular. An even smaller fraction of those are aerobic–utilize oxygen the way we do. And the tiniest percentage of those, have any form of neuron system for impulses and decision making. Intelligence is rare.*

Very rare, another agrees, gills flaring.

"But we are here," you say slowly, "and you exist too. That's two types of species in the universe that evolved separately! This is an incredible discovery for humans. It will change the world!"

One of the aliens leans back in an obviously surprised gesture. *Two organisms?*

We have discovered 14,482 species throughout the universe capable of nuclear fission, the head alien says. *Very rare indeed.*

"Fourteen thousand–what! That's not rare at all!" Craig says.

That is only 0.000000421 percent of all life in the universe, the alien responds. *And only 0.00000000000002 percent of all stars contain any life at all.*

Very rare indeed, the other two aliens say in your mind simultaneously.

"Oh," Craig says.

"So these tests," you say. "You were trying to gauge how smart we were?"

Yes. Your species has been broadcasting radio waves for 100 of your planet's years. You discovered the power of nuclear fission less than 50 years after that! Your rate of progress was astounding.

152

"Yet that wasn't enough?" Craig asks. "You had to make us go through mazes and other quizzes to figure us out?"

Many species we have discovered in the universe are strange. Some communicate via radio waves and visible light, yet have no fundamental intelligence. There is a type of insect on your planet that emits visible light that meets this description.

"Fireflies," you realize.

Yes. They emit parts of the electromagnetic spectrum, yet possess no intelligence. We send scouting ships with fabricated test facilities to these worlds to more accurately gauge their capabilities.

The alien behind you walks around. *We had trouble with communication when we neared your planet. You have thousands of different languages. Too many for a single species.*

Far too many. Our computer algorithms struggled, the head alien says. *We are lucky to be communicating at all. The tests and puzzles we fabricated based on your forms of entertainment.*

Video simulation games, the other says. *Television movies. Physical puzzles.*

"That explains a lot," Craig says. "Probably got the maze idea from the movie *Labyrinth...*"

"Wait a second," you say. "So we passed through the domes, taking your tests and helping you gather data on us. But when we were scanned by the computer here in the control room, it said there was a malfunction. That's why you were woken from your hibernation. Right? So what was the malfunction?"

One of the aliens turns around and examines the computer. It seems as though your question suddenly reminded them of that fact.

The aliens are silent as they look at the data. Their gills flare up every few seconds, and you get the impression they're having a discussion you cannot hear. Or an argument.

How is this possible? comes the voice in your head. Accusingly.

"How is what..."

These results are impressive. Out of 14,482 species discovered, none have showed proficiency in three skills!

You give a noncommittal shrug. "We're a pretty impressive species, for the most part. When we're not trying to kill one another."

They don't laugh at the joke. *This level of evolution is fascinating,* the head alien says. *You are equal to our species!*

"I'm not sure I'd go that far," Craig says, rubbing the back of his head. "You guys have spaceships that can visit other stars!"

Your species has a method of cooling itself by secreting liquid on your surface. Our species cannot do that.

You wipe your forehead. He's talking about sweating! "Yeah, I guess that's an advantage for humans. Especially while hunting. We could cool ourselves while moving, which most mammals cannot."

Mammals, the alien thinks, almost tasting the word.

"Oh, yeah," you say, trying to think of a way to explain it. "Mammals are a type of evolutionary branch here. The have mammary glands to feed their young, and reproduce by..."

We must bring a sample back.

The thought alarms you. It takes you a moment to realize what it means. "A sample of what?"

One of you. We must bring you back to our homeworld. You are unique!

You put up your hands. "Hey now. We did your tests, let us leave!"

But the aliens are all standing up now, in a semicircle around you and Craig. You feel like animals at the zoo again. You can feel the aliens' eagerness. Like you're a prize they've discovered.

154

"I'll go," Craig says.

"No!" you blurt out. "You don't have to do this! We can't–"

He cuts you off with a hand. "No, Jessica. I want to go. This would be the experience of a lifetime!"

You open your mouth to argue, but realize he's genuine. He seems downright excited by the idea! "Are you sure?"

"More sure than anything in my life! I have a desk job, Jessica. I'm a paper pusher. That's why I found every excuse I could to come out here and travel down to the habitat on the subs. I want to do something exciting for a change. And what's more exciting than traveling to an alien civilization?"

Navigating across the event horizon of a black hole, one of the aliens answers. You ignore it.

"What about everything back here on earth?"

Craig shrugs. "I'm not married. I have a sister who lives in Montana, but she has her own life. She'd be excited for me!"

You begin to realize just how serious he is. He really wants to do this. And nothing you say can convince him otherwise.

You turn to the aliens. "You'll take care of him? You won't dissect him to figure out how his insides work?"

The feeling of humor trickles into your mind, and you get the sense that the aliens are laughing. *Of course not. Only primitive species need to kill a creature to understand it.*

You decide not to tell him you dissected animals in graduate school. "Okay," you say to Craig. "If that's what you want to do, I won't stop you."

"You're sure you don't want to come too?"

You consider it, but only for a moment. It would be the experience of a lifetime, but it's not what you want for your future. You're happy to let Craig go, and are content knowing you represented humanity well in the testing domes.

"Yeah," you say with a smile. "I'm sure."

We must depart at once, the alien says. The others all move to the desks, suddenly preoccupied with their duties. *It will take approximately 4.367 of your planet's years to reach our system...*

"Wait, you mean you don't have warp technology?" Craig asks.

Our warp capabilities are reserved for emergency situations only. Such as a quick strike protocol against a hostile force.

Quick strike? You decide you're glad you don't qualify as a hostile force!

We will deposit you in your surface vessel, another says, this time to you. *Unless you would prefer a different location. Choose quickly.*

You smile.

Is this the end? *TURN TO PAGE 192*

156

From the descent, you didn't really get a good view of just how big the domes were, but now that you're inside it's clear: the domes are *enormous*. It's like being in the center of a football stadium, but without all the seats. The dome walls are almost entirely glass, hundreds of large triangles, with black girders spiderwebbing in between them for framework. The glass seems to give off light, so much that you realize you're squinting while your eyes adjust. Above and to your right you see a swarm of jellyfish float by. For a few minutes there you forgot you were at the bottom of the ocean!

"Wow," Craig says, drawing the word out into three syllables. "I've seen pictures, but they do not do it justice. Not at all."

You lower your gaze to the center of the room. It's flat and featureless, except for three glowing circles in the floor, arranged in a triangle formation. One circle is green, and has a small table in the middle, and the other two are red and empty.

Beyond that is a door marked DOME FOUR. Whatever those circles are for, it's not necessary. You need to get to Dome Three. You head in that direction until Craig grabs your arm.

"The door won't open unless we complete the tests."

"You mean you don't have some master unlock command, or something?"

He makes a weird face. "That would make things easier, wouldn't it?"

You take a long look at him. "Why do I get the feeling that *this* is a test?" He begins to protest, but you're already walking toward the door.

Sure enough, it doesn't open. And there aren't any handles or consoles to open it yourself.

"Fine, we'll do the test," you say, making it clear that you're not happy.

Craig shrugs. "I wish it were simpler, believe me!"

You approach the green ring. As you near, you see that there's a chess set on the table.

"Chess? That's the test?" you say.

A soothing voice cuts the air, robotic and calm. It seems to come from *inside* your head:

"*Checkmate the enemy player in one turn to advance.*"

"It's gotta be the white Queen we move," Craig says. "But which way do we move it to get checkmate?"

Do you know how to play chess? If not, ask a friend!

To move the white Queen vertically, *TURN TO PAGE 122*
If you want to move the white Queen diagonally, *GO TO PAGE 97*
Or, to move the white Queen horizontally, *SLIDE TO PAGE 52*

If you don't know, flip the table by *JUMPING TO PAGE 145*

158

You place the wire cutters around the second wire. You flinch as you squeeze the grip.

SNIP.

The timer begins counting down rapidly, beeping with every numeral.

"It didn't work!"

There's only 60 seconds left, and they're counting down *really* quick. Thinking fast, you close the box and grab the handle. Doing your best discus thrower impersonation, you spin around twice and hurl the bomb across the room. It bounces once, then twice, before coming to rest against the door marked DOME FOUR.

KABOOM!

You shield your face with your hands, but the explosion isn't very large. Beyond some pressure in your ears, you don't feel affected at all. As the smoke clears you see that the dome is still intact.

But the door to Dome Four is busted open.

You rub the back of your neck. "I'm going to pretend like I meant to do that."

Craig is still blinking rapidly, trying to regain his focus. "Oh. Yeah, wow. That was lucky, wasn't it?"

You're not sure how you cut the wrong wire, but it worked out in the end anyways. Feeling good, you walk into the tunnel.

Time to explore Dome Four *ON PAGE 140*

You press the Automatic Repair button. You doubt it will do much: Dome Three was practically torn in half!

All of a sudden, everything becomes transparent: the ceiling, the walls, even the door to Dome Three. You can see everything around you with crystal clarity, which for a brief moment is frightening. Now it *really* feels like you're standing at the bottom of the ocean!

You see dark objects inside the dome–what kind of tests await you inside?–but your attention is quickly pulled above that. The top of the dome, along the damaged edge, begins to glow faintly blue. The color intensifies and brightens. You can see the entire outline of the ruined dome perfectly.

Then everything changes.

Have you made a huge mistake? *TURN TO PAGE 109*

160

You take a moment to examine the board, visualizing the result of each option. Finally you nod to Craig and point to a square.

"There. I'm certain."

He must trust you, or else you sound awfully confident, because he moves his hand–and the hologram triangle–toward the square you chose. The mirror is sucked onto the square like a magnet, snapping into place. Immediately, the blue laser fires again.

PEW!

It ricochets off one mirror, than another, bouncing around at right-angles faster than you can blink. After completing its complicated route around the puzzle the beam strikes the blue circle on the right side. It makes a satisfying *DING* sound.

"Woohoo!" Craig says. "Way to go, Jessica!"

Before you have time to celebrate, the screen flickers. The laser grid stays the same, but all the other parts change: the mirrors and blocks shift, and move, and rearrange, until you're looking at a completely different puzzle.

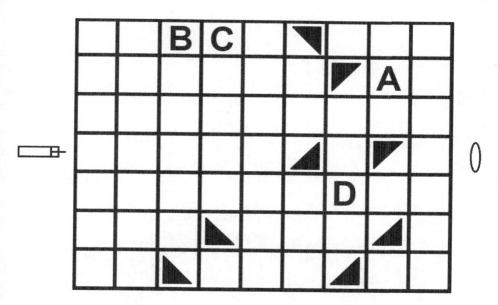

This time, a hologram of a triangle appears in *your* hand. You stare at it uncomprehendingly.

"I guess we have to solve another one?" Craig says.

Where do you place the mirror?

To place it in square **A**, *GO TO PAGE 131*
To place it in square **B**, *GO TO PAGE 114*
To place it in square **C**, *GO TO PAGE 118*
To place it in square **D**, *GO TO PAGE 137*

"It's a bomb!" Craig says. "What kind of a test is this!"

You examine the bomb. For some reason, the six wires on the top seem most important to you. Maybe you've seen too many action films.

Craig holds up a pair of wire cutters. "I think we need to use these. But which wire do we cut? Some of them are white with black stripes, others are black with white stripes. Some have no stripes at all!"

You notice words laser-etched into the side of the pedestal. At first they seem to be in a hundred different languages–French, and German, and some sort of symbol-based language–but as you squint they materialize into English.

Not odd stripes

Nor an odd wire

Not the wires white

Two stripes only–cut to retire

"I think it's a set of instructions," you say. "To defuse it!"

The wire cutters are trembling in your hand. What's it going to be?

To cut the first wire, *GO TO PAGE 167*
To cut the second wire, *GO TO PAGE 158*
To cut the third wire, *GO TO PAGE 132*
To cut the fourth wire, *GO TO PAGE 102*
To cut the fifth wire, *GO TO PAGE 95*
To cut the sixth wire, *GO TO PAGE 81*

164

"Clockwise," you immediately say. "There are five gears, so the odd ones will all rotate the same. Since gear one is clockwise, so is gear five!"

Your logic is correct, but instead of the sound of affirmation, there's a deep rumbling sound. A square door opens in the floor, clinking with the sound of hidden gears. A silvery pole rises out of the floor, no thicker than an umbrella rod.

As soon as the pole is at eye-level, it stops. With horror you see a blue laser shoot out of the tip at both you and Craig. It happens so fast that you don't have time to react: you don't even scream. You just stand there while the laser taps across your forehead, and then, just as quickly as it began, it stops.

The pole descends back into the floor. You blink and look around.

"What happened?"

As you turn to face Craig, you see a symbol burned onto the skin of his forehead. It glows softly.

You describe it to Craig, and he nods and confirms: you have the same one on your forehead.

Climbing out of the pit in a daze, you see that the door to Dome Three is now wide open. The dark tunnel beyond beckons you.

"Okay then. I guess we made it," Craig says.

"I guess we did."

Approach Dome Three *ON PAGE 130*

The peacock room is identical to the previous one, except for one key difference: in the center of the room is a statue of a peacock, feathers arrayed like a fan. It's made of the same black, spongy material you've seen throughout the habitat.

"She's beautiful," Craig says.

"He."

"Pardon me?"

"Male peacocks are the ones with the beautiful feathers," you explain. Seeing the statue in black, without the color, makes you strangely sad. To cover it up, you examine the room. There are two directions you can go.

To the east is a door with a hawk carved over the door.

To the west is an unmarked door. You remember it leads to the maze entrance.

"Males are the pretty ones? That doesn't make sense," Craig mutters.

To move into the hawk room, *FLY TO PAGE 27*
To return to the maze entrance, *GO TO PAGE 128*

166

You examine the board, imagining where the laser will travel. You point to one spot.

"There. I think."

Hesitantly, Craig reaches forward with the hologram triangle. As his hand nears the square you chose, the mirror is *sucked* onto the board as if pulled by an invisible string. There's a moment where everything is still, and then the blue laser fires again.

PEW!

The laser shoots across the board, bouncing around at the speed of light. You follow the beam with your eyes...

...to where it turns downward, leaving the board and striking the floor by your feet.

Craig jumps in the air. "Oof! Almost got my shoes!"

"Aww man," you say.

The screen makes a decidedly negative noise, and the lights of the screen and platform go out. A voice calls out from some unseen speaker, which must be in the floor because it sounds like it's coming from all around you at once:

"Subject: failure. Proceed to next dome."

The door across the room opens.

"I thought we failed," you said.

"We did."

"But if we failed, and still get to proceed," you say, "then what would have happened if we *succeeded?*"

Craig shrugs and quietly leaves the platform. There's nothing to do but follow.

Walk to Dome Two by *FLIPPING TO PAGE 120*

You place the wire cutters around the first wire. You flinch as you squeeze the grip.

SNIP.

The timer begins counting down rapidly, beeping with every numeral.

"It didn't work!"

There's only 60 seconds left, and they're counting down *really* quick. Thinking fast, you close the box and grab the handle. Doing your best discus thrower impersonation, you spin around twice and hurl the bomb across the room. It bounces once, then twice, before coming to rest against the dome wall.

Uh oh.

KABOOM!

The blast throws you backwards and makes your vision go white. When your sight returns you see that the explosion has blown a hole open in the dome. Water pours inside, along with jellyfish and squid and every manner of fish.

The door to the previous tunnel is open. You and Craig rush inside and it closes behind you. But now you're trapped, and you've damaged part of the research habitat as well! This won't be a happy ending for you. In fact, this is definitely...

THE END

168

You press the Diagnostics Information button. "I bet we can get some good info here," you explain.

"Sounds good to me."

Text flies across the screen, this time all in English. It moves too fast for you to see much, but you catch a few words:

...number 8 configured for maze code...

...subject test completion...

...results adequate for species...

...without resistance...

Then the words are gone, replaced by the previous menu.

"I guess the computer is made for someone who can read much faster!" Craig jokes.

You don't laugh. You're beginning to grow impatient.

To Enable Automatic Repair, *GO TO PAGE 159*
Or, if you want to see what the Exit Ship button does, *MOVE TO PAGE 92*

You jerk your head to the right. "How about we go this way?"

Craig shrugs. "Works for me."

Walking on the ocean floor is like moving in slow-motion. You can feel the weight of a few thousand feet of water pressing down on you, looming overhead. It's a good thing you're a marine biologist, or the feeling might paralyze you with fear. Somehow Craig manages to keep moving without it affecting him, walking along the ever-curving edge of Dome Three.

You can't help but examine the sandy floor in front of you. You've never been this deep! You spot a hundred different kinds of creatures that make their home on the ocean floor. Everywhere your eyes look there's something different, some which you recognize and some which are completely alien. You wish you had a notepad, or a camera, or something to record what you're seeing!

You're so engrossed in the wildlife that you wander too far sideways, never seeing the danger ahead.

You take a step, and your foot doesn't hit ground. It keeps falling into open ocean. You've walked off the edge of a cliff!

Crying out, you flail with your arms. It's too late–you're already falling forward. The cliff is completely vertical! Your boots scrape against the wall but all that does is make you tumble.

"Jessica!" Craig calls. His voice is distant and helpless.

Hopefully fate is on your side! What city are you (the reader!) currently in?

If your city begins with a letter between A - J, *GO TO PAGE 180*

Or, if your city begins with a letter between K - Z, *FALL TO PAGE 29*

170

The laser moves across your forehead as it scans for symbols. It almost feels like it makes your skin tingle, but that's probably just your imagination.

The blue light cuts off with finality. The voice returns, with an almost pleased tone.

"Data analysis: complete. Primary species of planet 4815162342-C is primitive in nature and not deemed a threat to colonization."

"Primitive in nature?" you say out loud. You feel strangely offended. "That's not true. We..."

"Hey, look!" Craig points. "The elevator's back!"

Any offense you felt immediately drains away. It's time to go home!

Quick! Before it closes, *TAKE THE ELEVATOR TO PAGE 173*

"The wheels change direction each time," you say out loud. "There are five wheels, so there's five changes. Which means the last wheel is spinning *counter-clockwise*."

There's a pause. You can sense the computer system—or whatever it is—calculating your response. Deciding your fate.

"Incorrect. Test subjects: defective. Disposing."

"Disposing?"

The floor opens like a trap door, dropping you so fast your stomach flies up into your chest. You barely have any time to cry out when you hit something metal.

"Oof!"

You bounce off, then hit something else a few feet lower. The smell of rust and machine grease stings your nostrils. You realize you're falling through an immense system of gearworks, most the size of a car tire, but some as big as a house!

You try grabbing onto something to slow your fall, but it's useless. The best you can hope for is that you won't get crushed. What's all this machinery even doing down here? It's a question that will have to wait, since now you're at...

THE END

172

The elevator makes its descent into the deep unknown. You try to estimate how far you go: 60 feet. 70. It doesn't make any sense to you. Why would there be an elevator leading deep into the ocean floor?

What's the point?

Without warning, the door opens. You didn't realize it had stopped–it was so smooth. Giving Craig a *this is your fault* look, you step out.

You're in a circular room. Platforms similar to desks are built into the walls, with what look like chairs spaced every few feet.

"It's like a control room," you say. "Or the bridge of an aircraft carrier."

Craig gulps as he looks around. "Yeah..."

There's a super-advanced looking computer screen to the left. To the right is what looks like an electronic map of some kind.

Weird. What do you want to examine first?

To check the computer screen, *GO TO PAGE 187*
If you want to survey the map, *TURN TO PAGE 63*

The elevator doesn't just go straight up. It lurches, moving sideways for ten seconds. Then it gently stops and begins ascending the way an elevator should.

When it opens, you're in a room you almost don't recognize. Craig does, though. "Hey! This is the docking structure at the center of the habitat!" He runs to the computer on the wall–which you now recognize as human technology, out of place with everything else you've seen. "Surface vessel, this is the research habitat. We need immediately extraction!"

The ten minutes waiting for the sub seem to last forever. Finally the hatch opens and the pilot waves you in.

"You okay, James?" Craig asks. "You look white as a ghost."

"Yeah, uhh... something has happened."

"What do you mean?"

He purses his lips. "Better for you to see for yourselves." He straps into the cockpit and begins leaving the habitat.

The night sky and open air are a welcome relief as the submarine surfaces. You bob in the water like a fishing float until the crane grabs you with its magnet and lifts you up.

Everyone is standing around on the deck of the RVS Aurora. "What's going on here?" Craig asks after you depart from the sub.

The Captain of the vessel doesn't even look in your direction. He merely points up to the sky. You follow his, and everyone else's, gaze.

The moon is a bright oval in the sky. It's different, somehow. The woman next to you hands you a pair of binoculars and you raise them to your eyes.

Lights. There are lights on the moon, hundreds of them, filling each visible crater like tiny domed cities. "They just arrived," the woman says, not taking her eyes off the satellite. "More ships come every ten minutes."

"What are they?" Craig asks.

You think you know the answer to that question. *Colonization.* In the coming days, months, and years, you'll learn more about the aliens. A *lot* more. But for now, all you know is that your actions in the habitat are responsible for this. You've doomed the human race. Think long and hard about that as you accept...

THE END

174

There's a long pause. You hold your breath, waiting for the response from the omniscient computer system.

> *"The primary species of planet 4815162342-C is adept in problem solving and logic. High potential for cooperative nodes."*

"Darn right we're good at problem solving," Craig says. You high-five his waiting palm. He adds: "Ohh. I get it! We were branded in Dome Two..."

There's a hum behind you. The elevator door has re-opened! You hesitantly move toward it, wondering if the computer will say anything else or try to stop you. It doesn't.

The elevator door closes, and then immediately opens. You're about to groan when you realize the view through the door is no longer the control room. You're in a circular room, with doors marked **Dome One, Dome Two**...

"This is the docking building," Craig says in awe. "We're back at the beginning!"

Craig presses the button to call the submarine. Immediately, the hatch opens and the pilot sticks his head inside.

"James! You were already waiting for us?" Craig says.

"Well..." James gets a funny look on his face. "Sorta had to. On account of the... well. You'll see." You and Craig share a worried look in the sub.

You breach the surface, and the sight of the research vessel through the bubbly window is a welcome sight. There's a *KA-CHUNK* as the crane magnet grabs the submarine and pulls up the side of the vessel.

You step out onto the deck, taking a deep breath of salty ocean air. It feels wonderful to be back!

Except for the two men in black suits and sunglasses approaching you. There's an ominous-looking government helicopter on the pad behind them.

"Miss. Kwon?" one of them says. Cautiously, you nod. "Please, come with us."

"Wait, what's the meaning of this?" you say. Craig looks between you and them as if wondering which side to take.

"It's classified. We'll explain on the way there."

Boy does *that* sound familiar. You consider arguing with them, but in the end go willingly.

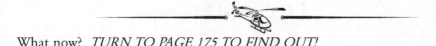

What now? *TURN TO PAGE 175 TO FIND OUT!*

Welcome to the White House!

You are JESSICA KWON, Chief Mediator for United States Extra-Terrestrial Relations. Strange ships from foreign star systems have landed all over Washington, made of the same spongy black material of the one at the bottom of the Pacific. Nothing has come out of them yet, but they've sent messages to the Congress and the President. The tests were to help the aliens figure out what humans were like. And apparently? They're impressed. They want to have a meeting to discuss peaceful diplomacy.

And they're asking for *you.*

It's not what you wanted to do in life. You're a *marine* biologist, not an alien biologist! But how could you say no? You were the first human to succeed in the alien habitat at the bottom of the Pacific Ocean. You're the only person for the job.

Well, not *just* you.

"I bet they have tentacles," Craig says. He's also a Mediator for the new government department, although one rank below you. He adjusts the badge on his suit. "Aliens always have tentacles."

"The odds of that are very low," you say. "Out of the billions of species on earth, how many have tentacles?"

He's unfazed by your logic. "If they have tentacles, how do we shake their hands? Do we bow? Or salute? Oh man..."

You're on the steps of the U.S. Capitol Building, surrounded by a dozen secret service members with earpieces. They seem twitchy today. Can you blame them? You're about to make first contact!

The alien ship sits on the lawn of the National Mall like some oval-shaped piece of modern art. A door opens from the seamless exterior, creating a rectangle of light. A gasp goes up from the crowd all along the barricades. A shadow moves inside the door!

You take a step forward.

Everything's going to change from this point on. The world will never be the same! And you're at the heart of it. It's not what you expected, but it's definitely...

THE END

176

You sprint down the corridor through the alien ship. The alarms pierce your ears like needles, giving you a constant, pulsing headache.

There are aliens out to get us, the thought floats through your head. *Heck, there are aliens, period!*

Craig takes one random turn, then another. The ship is massive. Your brain tries to picture its size relative to the research habitat and fails. How could something be so huge? That terrifies you more than the thought of aliens.

As you run through the ship, signs that it's coming to life are everywhere. Lights in the floor turn on, illuminating the path in too-bright light. Computer screens in front of doorways flicker on and display options in an alien language like Egyptian hieroglyphs. There's a growing vibration in your feet, as if a giant hummingbird is in the ship.

Through it all the alarm continues blaring, a constant reminder that you're an intruder in a hostile place.

"Where are we going?" you shout above the din.

"I don't know!" Craig yells. "I don't exactly have much experience exploring alien spacecraft!"

It's tough to gauge your location, but it feels like you're heading deeper into the ship. Farther away from the elevator and escape. "We can't keep running randomly," you say.

"I know," Craig says as he rounds a corner. "But we have to–"

You almost crash into him as you come around the edge. He's stopped in the middle of the hall, leaning back slightly.

Your eyes widen at the sight before you.

What is it?
Find out by *LOOKING TO PAGE 98*

You stare at the screen. It shows the view of another room, where a row of glass pods lean diagonally against a wall. Light glows from behind them, illuminating the occupants. Occupants with long limbs, and skulls shaped like jelly beans...

"Are those... *aliens*?"

Craig moans. "Frank, one of the astrobiologists, had a theory. Everyone thought he was crazy!"

"Craig, *are those aliens?*"

"We had no idea where these domes came from," he continues. He's talking to himself more than you. "The government just *found* them down here. They assumed it was an old Soviet station, even though the Russians denied it. None of the experts we brought in could explain any of it, and the weird tests..."

You feel your heart racing. Your brain struggles to process what you're looking at. "This has to be a prank," you say. "Or some sort of psychological test. Right? This can't be real."

"I want to go home," Craig says. "I didn't want to be here in the first place."

"You brought me here," you say, jabbing a finger at his chest. "You had no idea what this place was, and you brought me here anyways!"

Your flight-or-fight instinct kicks in, and flight wins. It's time to get out of there. You whirl around...

...only to find that the elevator is gone. There's only a smooth wall behind you.

"No!" you say, pounding on the alien desk. Suddenly the strange black material throughout the habitat makes more sense. "I have to get out of here! I'm a university professor! I'm the Dean!"

Horror is plastered to Craig's face. He's not going to be any help.

You look all around. There, in the corner to the right. There's a red circle glowing in the floor just like all the testing stations in the domes.

If you want to enter the circle, *STEP TO PAGE 129*
If you'd rather not, then instead *GO TO PAGE 103*

178

You hold your breath while waiting for the computer to continue. Next to you, Craig is doing the same.

"The primary species of planet 4815162342-C is skilled in mathematics and knowledge of astrophysics. Subject assistance on home planet is recommended."

"Yeah!" Craig says, pumping his fist. "You hear that? An *alien species* thinks we're skilled at math! That's impressive, right? It must be because we were branded in Dome Four. The one with the mathematics problems and questions about Jupiter. We *rocked* those."

"That's not the part that stuck with me," you say. "What did it mean by assistance on home planet?"

Without warning, a high-pitched whine sounds beneath you, like a jet engine spinning up. The room shakes violently, throwing Craig to the ground. You steady yourself on a nearby desk and help him up.

"What's happening?" you ask.

The computer must have somehow heard you. Though devoid of emotion, the words chill you to the bone.

"Exploratory ship mission is complete. Departing planet 4815162342-C immediately."

Craig's face is a mask of horror. "Exploratory ship? *What* exploratory ship?"

You soon find out. The far wall of the control room warps, like tinted glass suddenly losing its tinting. It shows the ocean floor beyond, sandy and covered with a hundred different crawling creatures. The sand falls away beneath you, but of course that's just what it *looks* like from your perspective. In reality, you're rising.

"I think *this* is the ship," you say. "The research habitat is one giant spacecraft!"

Craig doesn't have time to argue. Within seconds the ship has reached the surface, breaking through the water emphatically. The sunset on the horizon throws orange and pink across the sky. You see the surface vessel bobbing from the waves. Crew scramble to get control of the helicopter sitting on the pad, which rocks dangerously. All the people suddenly stop and stare up at the alien spaceship as if frozen in place. Soon they're nothing more than specks.

"Goodbye," Craig says with his face pressed against the glass. He waves down at the boat.

His lack of panic surprises you. "Are you okay?" you say. "I know I'm in shock right now. This doesn't seem real."

"You know what? I think I'm fine." He nods to himself. "Yeah. This is going to be an adventure. I've always wanted to do something fun and exciting, which is why I took the submarine down to the habitat–err, the spaceship. Can you imagine what we'll see?"

You watch the sun on the horizon as the spaceship rises into the atmosphere. It occurs to you that it might be the last time you *see* the sun. Soon you'll be in a different solar system. Maybe even a different galaxy!

Minutes later, earth falls away and an endless spray of stars appear. They're so bright from up here! You wonder which one is home to the aliens. Part of you is as excited as Craig, but the rest is disappointed. You're a marine biologist! There was so much more you wanted to learn on earth. You take a deep breath and let it out in a sigh as you accept that this is not your ideal version of...

THE END

180

You fall, and fall, and fall, and *fall*. Ocean particles move past your headlight, the only evidence that you're moving. Craig calls out to you, but soon his voice grows dimmer. Eventually it stops completely as you get out of range.

A grey wall appears out of the darkness, rushing toward you. There's just enough time to throw up your hands as you slam into it.

THWUMP.

Your body aches from the landing, but not very much. For a few seconds you lay there, staring at the sand particles pressed against your faceplate.

You push to your feet. The ground here is featureless: uniform grey in all directions. You can't even see the cliff wall. You have no idea how far you fell, but it must have been a long way.

Tilting your head up, you scan the water above you. There's nothing at all, just the same hazy water with a million particles floating in it. You can't see the research habitat, or the surface, or anything else.

You're all alone.

You wander the ocean floor, hoping to find some means of returning to the surface. You can't float up there because your suit weighs too much, and taking it off would be a *very* bad idea. Eventually your helmet light goes out. You sit down on the ground and stare off into the black.

Maybe Craig will get to the submarine, and pilot it down to search for you. You wonder how much air the suit has. Hopefully it's enough. But whatever happens to you, this is a dark and lonely way of reaching...

THE END

You confidently move the Knight forward. "I do believe that's checkmate."

But the board disagrees. It flashes red around the border, and the voice returns:

"Subjects too arrogant for test. Apprehend for later indexing."

"Indexing? I'm not a library card!" you say to Craig.

But he looks terrified, and is glancing all around. You don't think he's the cause of this.

The pieces on the chess board begin to move. Two of the Bishops grow, first the size of cats, then as big as you! They each hold a long staff in their hand. One levels it at you, and the other aims at Craig.

Light begins to glow from the ends.

"Run!" screams Craig. He's already halfway to the door! You're going to need some luck...

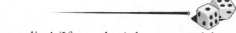

Roll two dice! (If you don't have any, pick a number between 2-12 randomly)

If you roll a 2, 3, 5, 6, 7, 8, or 11, *DUCK TO PAGE 74*
If you roll a 4, 9, 10, or 12, *SLIP TO PAGE 104*

182

The rumbling seems to draw closer as you wait, feet spread apart defensively. A thousand different scenarios flash through your mind, and none of them are good.

A wide door opens in the floor in the center of the room. A compartment like an elevator rises out of the ground, stopping silently. The side facing you is open and inviting.

"Well okay then," you mutter.

Craig shakes his head vehemently. "No. Absolutely not. I've had enough of all of this. Entering the domes was already too dangerous for an administrator like me. I'm certainly not going to be the one to explore further."

"Wait, what do you mean *explore*?" The fear on his face fills you with genuine worry.

"Nothing. All I mean is that..."

You grab his arm and spin him toward you. "No. Enough of this secrecy. I want answers, and I want them *now*."

Craig seems torn between wanting to say something and keeping his job. He furrows his brow and looks around for some other option.

"I... I can't, Jessica. If I do..."

It's enough. It's too much. Whatever is going on down here, with the domes and tests and *laser beams tattooing your forehead*, you're going to get answers.

And you're going to get them now.

"Let's go," you say, shoving Craig into the maybe-elevator. He cries out in protest but you step inside, blocking his escape.

"Please," he says. "You don't understand!"

"I will soon," you say, just as the doors close behind you. The elevator lurches and, after a brief pause, begins to descend.

Have you made a horrible mistake? Find out ON PAGE 172

184

"Data analysis complete," the soft, computer, *alien* voice announces. *"The primary species of planet 4815162342-C is adept in tactical logic. Although lacking long-term critical thinking, potential for future friction is high. Co-habitation unlikely."*

"What on earth does that mean?" Craig says. The voice chimes one last time before going silent.

"Recommended course of action: elimination."

"Okay, what does *that* mean?" he says.

You're afraid you know exactly what it means.

The elevator is suddenly back. You and Craig run inside, the doors closing behind you. It moves, and when the doors open you're some place different: back in the docking area.

Craig smashes the button to call the submarine. Nobody answers. "Come on, surface vessel. This is the research habitat. We need immediate extraction!" He turns to you. "Do you think... did we..."

"Did we what?"

"The alien voice said we lacked long-term critical thinking. Did we fail?"

You think about it for a moment. "We were branded at Dome One. With the hologram fighting and the laser puzzle. Tactics instead of strategy."

"Yeah, but did we *fail?*"

"Don't you see? There was no passing or failing. The aliens were testing us. To see what we–*humans*–were like!" You examine the computer panel. It's obviously human-made, and sticks out in the otherwise alien habitat. "Let me see if I can hack into this..."

"I thought you were a marine biologist?"

"I am," you say as you remove the panel, revealing the wires behind. "But I've been on a dozen expeditions where equipment has broken. You have to be your own IT person when you're alone on the coast of Tasmania."

The wiring is simple. Within minutes you've rerouted the signal to pick up other channels on the surface vessel. There's a crackle of static, and then sounds of mayhem.

"Hey, leave it there!" Craig says. "Oh no..."

You twist the two wires together and close the panel so you can see. It's a video feed from a news channel. The reporter is in Times Square, wind blowing her hair sideways. Behind her, people run in every direction.

The camera pans up. A dark circle blocks the sky, drifting slowly. The reporter manages to keep the panic out of her voice.

"As you can see, the unidentified flying object is more than five football fields long, with instruments that look like weapons on the underside. Already it has destroyed three passenger aircraft attempting to land at LaGuardia International Airport, with remaining craft grounded. Similar UFOs have been reported in Los Angeles, Tokyo..."

You slump to the ground in a heap, overwhelmed with what's happening. You sit there with your arms wrapped around your knees, not listening to the reporter anymore. All you and Craig can do is stare at the UFO on the screen, slowly blocking more and more of the sky as it descends on the city.

Somehow, this is your fault. You were representatives of mankind in the research habitat, and you failed! You're not sure what will happen to you and Craig, but for everyone else this is obviously...

THE END

186

"Let's get out of here!" you say, turning toward the door.

"But the bird..."

"I'd rather take my chances with it than the Pacific Ocean!"

The room is big. It's probably just the fear distorting things, but it seems to take you forever to run a few dozen feet. There's no sign of the ostrich in the hall beyond.

But it ends up not mattering. Just before you pass through the doorway, the walls seem to close in. The doorway narrows as the walls touch, blocking the way. It's as if there was never a door there to begin with.

"Oh no," Craig says.

"What happened? Is it sealing itself off against the leak?" Already there's a layer of water covering the floor.

"I don't know!"

"How do you not know? This isn't funny anymore, Craig! Tell me!"

He shakes his head. His skin is pale with fright. "This isn't our research habitat. We found it. I knew I should have stayed in my office today..."

You open your mouth to ask him what he means, but just then the wall of the dome bursts. Water gushes inside like a hundred firehoses, churning around your knees, then your waist.

This isn't what you expected when you decided to become a marine biologist.

Soon you're floating on the surface of the water, being carried toward the roof of the dome. There has to be a way out. Right? Some sort of safety mechanism. You're going to wonder in vain, however, because this is a watery version of...

THE END

You stride toward the computer screen. It's positioned over one of the weird desks, about a foot off the wall. Although you can see the faint glow indicating the power is on, it's currently blank.

There aren't any keyboards in the room, but this desk does have some indentations arrayed in a crescent shape. It looks like the paint easel your nieces use to finger-paint. Tentatively, you reach out to press one.

Nothing happens.

You touch another, then a third. It doesn't seem to be working. Frustrated, you press all ten of your digits on the not-keys as if you're banging on a piano.

There's a soft vibration in your left pinky finger, sort of like the sensation of touching a plasma globe. You pull your hand back, then press just that key with your index finger.

You flinch as the computer screen turns on, so bright that you need to cover your eyes with a hand. A dozen other rectangles of light flick on throughout the control room. It takes your eyes a moment to adjust. You squint at the one directly in front of you.

Your jaw drops. It can't be!

"Oh my god," you say.

"What is it?" Craig comes jogging over. "Oh. Oh no..."

"Are those..." you ask.

Are those *what?* Find out ON PAGE 177

188

"Data analysis complete. The primary species of planet 4815162342-C is adept in strategic, long-term thinking. Danger in colonization. Return journey: initiated."

"Hey now, nobody here is a danger." Craig puts his hands up as if surrendering.

"I think it's because we completed Dome Five," you say. Your certainty grows with every word. "Strategic thinking. The chess puzzles, the map-related questions..."

"You're totally right!" Craig says. "We knew the domes were tests for humans, but we didn't know the purpose. They wanted to know how we think!"

The ground begins to tremble. Is it a deep-sea earthquake? Maybe that's what damaged Dome Three!

But something else is happening. The lights inside the control room begin turning on, flickering red and yellow in random synchronization. Data moves across one screen, but it's nothing you can read. The language looks distinctly alien, now that you know.

"What's happening?"

You shake your head. "I don't know!"

The earthquake feeling ends, but you can still feel something different. Like you're on a moving train but can't see the windows.

Everything grows blurry, like your eyes are watering. The colors and shapes all change and warp and twist...

...without warning, walls appear all around you. They're grey and metallic, familiar and foreign all at the same time. You blink away the blurriness and rub your eyes until everything makes sense.

"We're back on the surface vessel!" Craig shouts.

That's why it's all familiar. You're on the bridge of the surface vessel where the helicopter landed. Except...

"Where is everyone?" you ask.

Craig's smile disappears like it was knocked away with a baseball bat. He looks all around once, then a second time. "Uhh..."

You know this is bad. Why would the Captain—and all of the crew!—abandon their posts? Were they somehow teleported off the ship, the way you were teleported *onto* it?

Shouts outside are music to your ears. You and Craig rush out the door and onto the deck.

Everyone—the Captain, the crew, all the other scientists—are standing along the railing with their backs to you. Craig puts his hands on the shoulder of a man dressed all in white. "Captain? Hello?"

If the Captain is surprised to see you and Craig suddenly aboard, he doesn't show it. In fact, he doesn't say anything. All he does is point.

You look.

The water is rising in the distance like an enormous wave. The wave breaks, revealing the black, spongy material of the research habitat—or rather, the alien spaceship. The ship rises into the air and, with a shimmering whine of technologically advanced engines, shoots away into the sky. The rest of the water rains back down onto the ocean, and then everything becomes still.

Return journey: initiated. That's what it said, and suddenly it all makes sense. The aliens decided you were strategic and dangerous, so they're fleeing back home!

Craig lets out a sigh that's either relief or disappointment. Your own feelings match his. Did you luck out and avoid contact with a super-advanced civilization that could have vaporized all of you? Or did you miss out on the greatest discovery in the history of the world?

Maybe someday you'll know for sure. But that day is not today, for you have reached...

THE END

190

Craig decides for you. "I think this is the best way." His guess is as good as yours, so you nod and follow him to the left.

You can't help but stare intently at the sandy ground. Sand crabs and anemones and tiny shell-fleas–there's an entire ocean ecosystem down here! Under different circumstances you wish you could stop and watch for longer.

The two of you follow the curving dome around until another dome comes into view, bright and filled with, you know, *air*. You keep going until your path ends at the long tunnel connecting the domes together.

"I don't see any doors," Craig says. The headlamp on his suit pans over the exterior of the tunnel, black and featureless. You walk along the tunnel, waiting for some sort of airlock or hatch to appear. You begin losing hope.

Until a ladder mounted onto the outside comes into view. "Alright!" Craig says.

You climb the ladder to the top of the tunnel, then climb down another one on the opposite side. Since the research habitat is shaped like a wheel, with the domes on the outside, that puts you on the interior section. Where the docking building is. It's a dark blob on the ocean floor ahead of you.

"Now we just need to hope that–yeah!"

His headlamp stops on a rectangular outline, with yellow stripes painted against the black. Craig practically hops up and down with excitement. It's an airlock!

Like all the doors inside the domes, it opens automatically at your approach. You step inside the flooded room, which is just big enough for two people in those bulky suits. The door behind you closes, and the water immediately begins draining. You grin as the water line reaches your face.

The docking building is a welcome sight. Once inside, you practically rip off your suit. It opens at invisible seams and falls to the floor with a thump.

"Boy does it feel good to be out of that!"

Craig nods. He goes to the computer panel and types in a code. He examines the screen and pumps a fist. "Hello there, topside. This is the research habitat calling for immediate extraction. Over."

The response comes immediately. "Roger that, research habitat. Sending sub two now."

The wait is excruciating. You can't help but feel like something is going to go wrong. But this time nothing does, and the submarine docks with a soft *clang* sound. Craig spins the hatch open and you both hop inside.

"Get us out of here," Craig tells the pilot.

You put on your harness and melt into your seat back. Eventually you'll be debriefed, and maybe get more answers out of Craig regarding the purpose of the habitat, but for now you don't care. The mysteries of the murky deep will have to wait. You're going home, and that's all that matters. You've never been so relieved to have reached...

THE END

192

Welcome to Stanford University!

The campus is sprawled beneath you as you look down from the spaceship cockpit. You can see the students going about their day as if nothing is strange. *They cannot see our spacecraft*, the alien pilot says inside your mind.

"Can you change that?" you ask.

If you wish.

You turn to Craig, and give him a long hug. The two of you have been through a lot in the past few hours. There's no need to say anything, though. You both understand.

Stand inside the blue circle and we will transport you down.

You do as you're told. Your skin begins to vibrate, as if all the atoms are slowly coming apart. It doesn't hurt, though, and after seeing the alien technology you trust it completely.

"Goodbye," you say, both to the aliens and Craig. "Have a safe trip!"

Craig grins, then turns to the aliens. "Hey, so why did you land in the bottom of the ocean, anyways?"

The alien stares at Craig as if it's a stupid question. *Your planet is 71 percent water. Why would we assume the dominant species is not water-based?*

It's the last thing you hear, and then the ship is gone.

You're floating through the air, high above the university. You're unafraid. Students down on the campus lawn are pointing in the air, some of them crying out in surprise. You look up and see the alien ship in its full size. It's like a city of black metal floating in the sky. One of the domes is barely visible, reflecting the afternoon sun. Slowly, as if it were a mirage, the ship disappears.

You wave goodbye one final time before turning your gaze downward.

A crowd of students watches as you drift to the ground, gently coming to a stop in front of the biological sciences building. You take a deep breath and brush off your clothes.

"Well?" you say to the gaping students. "What's the problem? You all studied for the midterm, right?"

You stride inside the building, grateful that they can't see your smile. Part of you wished you had gone with Craig to the alien world, but it's only a small part. This is where you belong. You open the doors to your auditorium, inhaling the oaken smell. Maybe you'll see Craig again in the future, but that's another adventure for another time.

You completed the tests! Found the alien spaceship! And returned home in one piece!

CONGRATULATIONS!
YOU HAVE REACHED THE ULTIMATE ENDING!

In recognition for taking up the gauntlet, let it be known to fellow adventurers that you are hereby granted the title of:

Oceanic Alien Arbitrator

You may go here: **www.ultimateendingbooks.com/extras.php** and enter code:

SH10379

for tons of extras, and to print out your Ultimate Ending Book Ten certificate!

And for a special sneak peek of Ultimate Ending Book 11, *TURN TO PAGE 195*

194

The laser scans your forehead. In less than a second it's done.

"Scanning error."

"Uhh, what?" you say. Craig shrugs.

"Insufficient data present. Eliminating biological contamination."

"What's that mean?" Craig says. "Are we contaminated?"

A door opens up in the ceiling. A metal arm descends, with what looks suspiciously like a laser.

"Craig... I think we *are* the contamination! Or at least, that's what it thinks!"

You back away slowly. The tip of the laser begins glowing a malicious shade of crimson, altogether different than the blue laser you've seen throughout the facility. You put up your hands to protect yourself, a feeble, primitive gesture. It won't help you, because you've failed whatever test the aliens had for you. Close your eyes and accept that this is...

THE END

Welcome to the Antarctic Circle!

You are ALYSSA HILL, daredevil helicopter pilot and conquerer of six different continents (including this one). You've seen inclement weather and flown choppers in all kinds of conditions before, but nothing like this!

It's icy. It's windy. It's almost unflyable! And yet somewhere beneath your red and white Airbus H125, a vast landscape of snow spins out in every direction. Of course you can't see any of it through the storm, but the reliable panel of instruments at knee-level tell you it's there.

"Are you sure you're okay?" you ask for the fifth or sixth time. To your left, JONAS BENEDICT grips his seat with both hands.

"F-Fine," he assures you over the ever-present sound of the rotor blades. The man's fingers are white. The blood has long since left them. But it's the color of his face – a sickly, yellowish green – that worries you most.

"I told you, stop looking down. Look outside. Try to find the horizon."

"Really?" he chokes. Your companion's voice is short, his throat squeezed tight in an effort to keep his stomach in check. "In *this*?"

The world outside your canopy is a swirling mass of snow. It churns so quickly and in such random directions it's almost hypnotizing. For that reason, you keep your eyes locked squarely on your instrument panel. Here in the Antarctic, you know spatial disorientation accounts for more than half of all air accidents.

"Well do your best," you tell him. "We're almost there."

Jonas nods. It's about all he can do.

Truth be told, you're getting a little queasy yourself. You work hard to keep the stick steady as wind buffets your helicopter from every conceivable angle. It's not your first time in a storm. But it's your first time in an Antarctic blizzard, and that leaves every one of your senses in a heightened state of awareness.

The job was supposed to be easy: a quick run out to Drill Station 31. Your only cargo: one passenger, a VIP biochemist who needs to be rushed to the station 'as quickly as humanly possible'. Considering the magnitude of the impending storm that didn't make much sense. But the money was good and the route was simple, so you were more than happy to take the assignment.

"So why do they need you?" you ask.

Jonas swallows hard. It takes longer than normal. "What?"

196

"Well it's a drill station," you explain. "The Antarctic Ice Project does core samples, hundreds of feet into the ice shelf. Seems to me they'd need a geologist. Maybe a drill mechanic. Something like that."

"So?"

"So you're a *biochemist*. Why would they need–"

A light on your panel suddenly blinks off. You toggle a switch back and forth but nothing happens.

"That's strange."

Jonas looks up slowly, his face still green. "What is?"

"The station's VOR beacon. It's gone dark."

"The VO-what?"

"The navigational beacon. It was there a second ago, but now it's switched off."

You flip your radio to the station's frequency and thumb the mic. "Drill Station thirty-one this is 8081 Sierra Bravo. GPS reads us four miles out. VOR is non-responsive, please advise."

The only answer you get is static. That, plus the howling of the wind outside.

"Drill Station thirty-one, do you copy?"

Two minutes later you've tried four other channels, including all the localizer frequencies. Even so, you get no response.

Jonas shoots you an uneasy glance. Now he looks queasy *and* concerned. "So... so we can't find the station?"

"Nonsense. The GPS still works and I've got the coordinates already programmed." You check the panel. The distance to the station is steadily ticking down. "We're locked in. We'll just have to come in slow."

Your passenger breathes a sigh of relief. "Slow sounds good."

A gust of wind drives your nose up. You push forward on the stick, smooth and slow, fighting it down.

"Why aren't they answering?" you ask Jonas. "Who monitors the radio?"

Your passenger shrugs. "No clue. It's my first time here."

Down below, the station remains eerily silent. Even the landing assistance systems appear to have been switched off.

"We should see lights by now," you say. "Hand me that map."

Jonas reaches over and grabs a large piece of paper. He unfolds it, revealing a broad, pencil-drawn sketch:

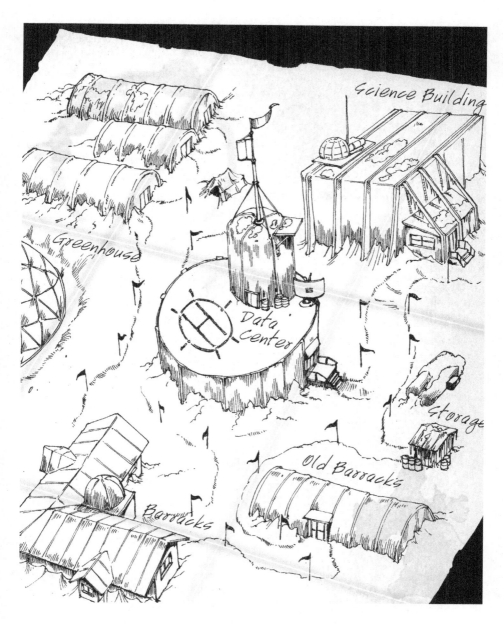

198

"That's not a map," Jonas says. "It's a drawing!"

"A sketch of the base, yes."

"You drew this?"

"I wish," you answer. "No, this my first time here too. The Danforth corporation found this sketch among the last pilot's belongings and thought I could use it. Right after he mysteriously quit working for them."

When it comes to the Danforth corporation you know very little, only that they own and operate the drill station. You know even less about Futuro, the company that paid you a very pretty penny to fly Jonas Benedict out here.

"So if you already know the coordinates, why do you need the sketch?"

"Well," you reply with a smirk, "when flying somewhere new, I kinda like to know where I'm supposed to land."

Jonas doesn't have much to say after that. You continue descending through the storm, grateful for the silence.

"Keep an eye peeled for the DME antenna," you say. "There should be some sort of spire with a blinking ligh–"

POP!

A small explosion rocks the chopper! It seems to have come from somewhere overhead...

"What in the–"

WHIIIIIIRRRRRRRRR...

Your stomach drops into your feet as you recognize the sound. It's the whir of the engine winding down!

"What happened?" shouts Jonas. "What happened!"

"The engine just went out."

"What? *HOW?*"

"Don't know yet," you say calmly. "Stand by."

"St–Stand by? You want me to *stand by?*"

You scan the instrument panel left to right. Mechanically your hands begin flipping a series of switches.

"We're in trouble," you tell Jonas. For some reason, time seems to slow down. Images of an emergency landing flash through your mind. Adrenaline surges through your body, bringing everything into sharp focus.

"Well what do we do?" your passenger pleads.

"The way I see it we've got two choices," you say quickly. "First, I can attempt to restart the engine–"

"That sounds good!" Jonas interrupts.

"–but if that doesn't work, we're in a much worse situation than before. We'll have lost a lot more altitude."

Jonas gulps.

"Or?"

"Or I set the rotors to neutral and we auto-rotate down."

"Auto-what?"

"We set the bird free. Let the free air moving up through the rotors generate enough lift to get us down."

"Will that work?"

"In theory, sure," you say. "But..."

"But you've never tried it."

"Not in a landing sense, no."

The rotors are slowing down now. You can almost see them. The roar of the storm grows louder with every passing second...

Will you be able to land safely and aid the...

CRISIS
AT
DESOLATION
STATION

ABOUT THE AUTHORS

David Kristoph lives in Fort Worth, Texas with his wonderful wife and two not-quite German Shepherds. He's a fantastic reader, great videogamer, good chess player, average cyclist, and mediocre runner. He's also a member of the Planetary Society, patron of StarTalk Radio, amateur astronomer and general space enthusiast. He writes mostly Science Fiction and Fantasy. www.DavidKristoph.com

Danny McAleese started writing fantasy fiction during the golden age of Dungeons & Dragons, way back in the heady, adventure-filled days of the 1980's. His short stories, The Exit, and Momentum, made him the Grand Prize winner of Blizzard Entertainment's 2011 Global Fiction Writing contest.

He currently lives in NY, along with his wife, four children, three dogs, and a whole lot of chaos. www.dannymcaleese.com

Printed in Great Britain
by Amazon

22504355R00116